Basheer

... well worth possessing. *– The Business Standard*

This anthology by Katha traverses the entirety of Basheer's planet of diverse people and conflicting emotions.

– The Express Magazine

The book contains twelve of Basheer's immortal stories, each a gem and a classic by itself ... The aesthetically designed and almost flawlessly printed book is a must for all those who are lovers of the exquisite and the brilliant in Indian literature. Competent translations add to the the pleasure.

– The Hindustan Times

I congratulate Katha and its chief architect, Geeta Dharmarajan, for their missionary zeal in discovering creative talent in India's varied languages ... the publishers have made it into a beautiful book, pleasing to the eye and challenging to the discriminating reader.

– Indian Review of Books

OUR RECENT RELEASES

Short Fiction

Katha Prize Stories 10
    Ed. Geeta Dharmarajan
    & Nandita Aggarwal
Hauntings: Bangla Ghost Stories
    Edited and Translated by
    Suchitra Samanta
Forsaking Paradise: Stories from
Ladakh, Edited and Translated by
    Ravina Aggarwal
Ayoni and Other Stories
    Edited and Translated by
    Alladi Uma & M Sridhar
Home and Away
    By Ramachandra Sharma
    Translated by Padma and
    Ramachandra Sharma
Vyasa and Vighneshwara
    By Anand
    Translated by Saji Mathew
Joginder Paul: Sleepwalkers
    Translated by Sunil Trivedi and
    Sukrita Paul Kumar

ALT (Approaches to Literatures in Translation)

Ismat: Her Life, Her Times
    Eds. Sukrita Paul Kumar &
    Sadique
Translating Partition: Stories, Essays, Criticism
    Eds. Ravikant & Tarun K Saint
Vijay Tendulkar

Trailblazers

Paul Zacharia: Two Novellas
    Translated by Gita Krishnankutty
Ashokamitran: Water
    Translated by Lakshmi Holmström
Bhupen Khakhar: Selected Works
    Translated by Ganesh Devy,
    Naushil Mehta and Bina Srinivasan

Indira Goswami: Pages Stained with
    Blood, Translated by Pradip Acharya

Katha Novels

Singarevva and the Palace
    By Chandrasekhar Kambar
    Translated by Laxmi
    Chandrashekar
Padmavati
    by A Madhaviah
    Translated by Meenakshi
    Tyagarajan

YuvaKatha

Lukose's Church
Night of the Third Crescent
Bhiku's Diary
The Verdict
The Dragonfly
The Bell

BalKatha

The Carpenter's Apperentice
The Nose Doctor
Grinny the Green Dinosaur
Battling Boats

FORTHCOMING

Pudumaippittan: Fictions
    Edited and Translated by
    Lakshmi Holmström
Ai Ladki
    By Krishna Sobti
    Translated by Shivnath
Daar se Bichchudi
    By Krishna Sobti
    Translated by Smita Bharti
Surajmukhi Andhere Ke
    By Krishna Sobti
    Translated by Pamela Manasi

SHORT STORIES

Basheer

VAIKOM MUHAMMAD

Edited by
Vanajam Ravindran

KATHA

First published by Katha in 1996

Copyright © Katha, 1996

Copyright © for each of the original stories is held by the author's family.

Copyright © for the English translations rests with KATHA.

KATHA
A-3 Sarvodaya Enclave
Sri Aurobindo Marg
New Delhi 110 017
Phone: 4141 6600, 2652 4511
Fax: 2651 4373
E-mail: kathavilasam@katha.org
Internet address: http://www.katha.org

KATHA is a registered nonprofit society devoted to enhancing the pleasures of reading.
KATHA VILASAM is its story research and resource centre.

Cover Design: Geeta Dharmarajan
Cover painting: Ramananda Bandopadhyay
Courtesy: Gallerie Ganesha

General series editor: Geeta Dharmarajan
In-house editors: Mridula Natha Chakraborty & Meenakshi Sharma

Design: Taposhi Ghoshal
Illustrations: Paul Kallanode

Typeset in 10.5 on 13.5pt Bodoni by Suresh Sharma at Katha.
Printed at Ana Print O Grafix Pvt. Ltd., Greater Noida (UP).

Distributed by KathaMela, a distributor of quality books.
E-mail: marketing@katha.org

Katha has planted a tree to replace the wood used in the making of this book.

ISBN 978-81-87649-52-6

4 5 6 7 8 9 10

Vaikom Muhammad Basheer
January 20, 1908 – July 5, 1994

Basheer working with the bare essentials

The Circle of Fiction

Basheer with wife Fatima Bi,
daughter Shahina Habib and Son Anees

Basheer at one of his favourite haunts

CONTENTS

PREFACE

Kudu vittu kudu payarathu
From one nest to another

Many, many years ago, I remember sitting with the Tamil version of *Vikramaditya*. Then, I didn't know it was a translation. Just that it was one of the most fascinating fantasies I could have laid my hands on. My mind lingered on every idea, every nuance, on every movement the king made when he left his body to enter that of another human being. And then the adventure would start ...

And now, once again, it is the old magic at work as I read Basheer. Only this time, it is as if I am in another's skin, having adventures that I, in my brahmin ignorance, never knew existed! Vaikom Muhammad Basheer reels out his extraordinary stories as if they are the most natural things ever to happen to human beings. They could have happened to anyone, he seems to say – as if he doesn't even think people like me could exist, timid people who lead vicarious lives. But then, maybe he did. Perhaps that is why he peopled his stories with such believable out-of-this-world characters who will live as long as there are readers to enjoy them and bring them to glorious life. For the few hours that the stories take to read, they take you to places the inveterate traveller Basheer has visited, making (I hope) each one of us a totally different person from the one who started reading the first page of this book.

Someone once said that there can be no majority in India. Each one of us belongs to some minority group.

by
Geeta Dharmarajan

Basheer, for instance, is from Kerala, one of the smallest states of India with one of the smallest populations. Add to this the fact that he is a Muslim. And, in translation, he moves into an even smaller minority! But Basheer, his inimitable eye observing everything and everyone, makes the state of being in a minority quite wonderful.

And perhaps, it is because of his minority status (not unlike that of Indian fiction in translation, which is still marginalized in India and abroad), that Basheer has a special role to play in freeing the imagination of Indians who read only in English.

The Katha Classics are a special series that aim to showcase the best of our writers of short fiction. The first volume of the series, *Masti Venkatesha Iyengar*, has been received well. We hope for an equally favourable response from you for this one, discerning reader.

For this book, I take pleasure in thanking our editor, Vanajam Ravindran, who went that extra bit to make it what it is. And the translators who have given us these sensitive translations. I thank Fabi Basheer for permission to translate and publish these stories and for the hospitality she so spontaneously showed to Vanajam. And M N Vijayan, for an insightful introduction to Basheer. I am very grateful to Adoor Gopalakrishnan for sending us at short notice stills from his film *Mathilukal* and to Punalur Rajan for allowing us to use some of his photographs.

I also thank Taposhi Ghoshal, our designer, Paul Kallanode, the illustrator, S Ganeshan, our production-in-charge, the in-house editors of this volume, Mridula Nath Chakraborty and Meenakshi Sharma, and the resource people, Josy Joseph and Swapna Jose. And the many others in Katha who were involved in the making of this book. I hope you enjoy Basheer in this translation and that it takes you speedily into other translations and other, still undiscovered, story-lands.

New Delhi
August 1996

EDITOR'S NOTE

On a sultry afternoon in February 1994, I set out for Beypore, accompanied by a photographer, to have some pictures taken of the octogenarian Beypore Sultan for the Katha Classics series. This sobriquet had stuck with Basheer ever since he once referred to himself as the Sultan of his two-acre land. Vylalil House, his residence, is as well-known in Beypore as its shipbuilding centre. A painful wheezing could be heard right at the gate. At the doorway, I saw someone who looked like a character out of a Beckett novel. A shrunken man, his torso bare, supporting himself on the knees and elbows, the very image of dotage and decrepitude. Fabi Basheer apologetically told us that her husband had had a bad night.

A week later, when he was relatively better, I made another trip to Beypore. This time to obtain translation rights from Basheer and to get him to talk. Surprisingly, he became alert when it came to business. He was the first Malayalam writer to demand adequate remuneration for writers. In *Kathabeejam*, a play based on Basheer's own experiences, a starving writer is told by an editor that the copyright of his stories rests with the publishers, who have not even paid him for his work. The editor argues that fame is reward enough for a writer. The impoverished and aggrieved writer then says, "People spend money on films, the theatre, cigarettes. But when it comes to reading, which is also a form of entertainment, they expect to get it free. The writer needs sustenance and space for writing. I am not talking about myself, but on behalf of all writers,

by
Vanajam Ravindran

men and women like me." But the outraged editor retorts, "I don't intend to make the sacred temple of Literature into a whorehouse!"

I asked Basheer if he subscribed to the notion of art for art's sake. His answer was a categorical "No." Despite his pragmatic views on the writer's profession and authorial freedom, Basheer nevertheless believed that the ultimate end of life and art was *Nanma* (goodness) – the betterment of the self and humanity.

Our conversation veered to intercommunity marriages and he said, "I almost married a Hindu Nair girl." But then, "Anuragathinte Dinangal" (The Days of Love), drawn on his passionate love affair may not have been written! Saraswathi Devi, a young college student and admirer of Basheer's work, was all set to flout social conventions to marry him. Her parents threatened to take their lives if their daughter married a Muslim. The idea of a togetherness with death looming large behind it was inconceivable to Basheer. He pleaded with Devi to forget him and marry the man of her parents' choice. The pain of this truncated experience took its toll on his mental well-being leading him to intemperance of an alarming nature.

His rather bohemian life-style came to an end only in his fiftieth year, when his well-wishers got him to marry the twenty-three-year-old Fatima Bi. Fabi, as Basheer fondly referred to her, soon became a sheet anchor to the wild impulses that ever so often clouded his reason.

But Basheer, like Dostoevsky, had the courage to face his disease and overcome it as best as he could. He writes, "I felt my mind bogged down by darkness, a darkness filled with terrifying dreams ... Oh, this abysmal darkness closes in on me from all the eight directions, roaring and thundering. Will I be drowned in this for ever? No, I will not allow my life to be shattered ... Let me muster all my strength, let me make one great effort to get well ... Let me not lose hold of reason. Let me find out the cause. Isn't there a cause for everything? Courage – let me courageously try to find out what is wrong."

Referring to his quirks, Fabi once told me how, in the early years of their marriage, she used to be intrigued by Basheer's long conversations with himself. He would not brook any interruptions, motioning her away whenever she approached him with a glass of tea or food. It did not take her long to understand that, on those occasions, he was narrating to himself entire stories that he would eventually write. Fabi mentioned another interesting facet of his personality – clairvoyance. He had once handed her some of his premonitory utterances jotted down in a diary saying, "Here's a gold mine for you. Keep it safe. Alas, the white ants have played havoc with it!"

During my last visit to the writer in late February 1994, we talked about religion and religious experiences. When I asked about the metaphysical despair and fear described in "Anarghanimisham" (The Invaluable Moment) and "Sandhyapranamam" (An Evening Prayer), his wizened face visibly lit up. Someone was taking the spiritual dimension of his writing seriously! On asking if these were drawn from felt experiences, he said "Yes." Soon, thereafter, out of concern for his weak health, I got up to leave, but he said, "Don't go as yet. I like listening to what you have been saying."

So we continued to talk and I told him about Cardinal Newman and T S Eliot and how they had spoken in the same vein of their experiences of the divine. He listened with interest and talked of his own stories. "Anarghanimisham" was the outcome of a sudden premonition of death one day. "I" was going to become extinct. This predilection for the spiritual was evident right from his early years, he said. He had savoured the tranquility of ascetic life when, as a wanderer in North India, he spent about three-and-a-half years in the company of Hindu sanyasis. Later, he had occasion to interact for about the same length of time with Sufis. For Basheer there was no conflict, only consanguinity, between the enlightened Hindu's notion of "Aham Brahmasmi" and that of "Anal Huq" (I am the truth) advocated by his Sufi brother. Despite the fascination asceticism held for him, he could not embrace it, being a man of action and a believer of the Quran, which advocates involvement in the world.

Basheer passed away on July 5, 1994 leaving behind his wife Fabi, daughter Shahina Habib and son Anees. He is known mostly for the three novellas – *Balyakalasakhi*, *N'te Uppooppakkoru Anadarnu* and *Pathummayute Adu* – and the stories "Mathilukal" (Walls) and "Viswavikhyatamaya Mookku" (The World-renowned Nose). These works are typical of the writer's genius insofar as they reflect his puckish humour, pungent satire, racy language, a tendency to debunk rhetoric and a propensity for descriptions of common life. Yet they do not fully reveal Basheer, the man and writer.

This volume is an attempt to offer a fuller portrait of the writer by including certain writings of his that suggest his preoccupation with man's existential problems and the distinction between good and evil. Even the Malayalam readers of Basheer seem to have paid scant attention to these concerns of a writer they held in high esteem. It is hoped that the present collection will enable the interested reader not only to hear the many voices of Basheer – that of the satirical humourist, the story teller par excellence, the anguished thinker and poet engaged with universal human problems – but also encourage students of fiction to undertake an in-depth study of the writings of one foremost in the sphere of the Malayalam short story.

I am deeply indebted to Sukumar Azhikode, K Satchidanandan, M M Basheer and R Viswanathan for their valuable suggestions regarding the translations. I thank M N Karasseri for helping with the bibliography and drawing my attention to the marked Sufi strains in Basheer's writings. I am also obliged to K G Karthikeyan of the Malayalam Departmental Library (Calicut University).

To Fabi Basheer I owe immense gratitude not only for her warm hospitality during my visits to Vylalil House but also for patiently answering all my queries. I am greatly indebted to K Devaki for clarifying endless doubts about the nuances of Malayalam words. And finally, I thank the Katha team without whose help and assistance these translations would not have been possible.

Kozhikode
August 1996

Introduction

More than five decades ago, Vaikom Muhammad Basheer altered the map of Malayalam fiction. Unknowingly. He, who was not quite sure of its alphabet, revolutionized the art of story telling in Malayalam. A radical change in the literary vocabulary was, in fact, essential to make Basheer's narratives work. Words drawn from the workaday world of common people became vibrant when he used them in a functional and seemingly artless manner.

Born probably on January 20, 1908, Basheer was the eldest of the six children of Kunhachumma and Kayi Abdu Rahiman, a prosperous timber merchant from Thalayolaparambu, a small village in Vaikom, Kerala.

By the age of eight, Basheer had completed his study of the Quran. After attending a primary Malayalam school in Thalayolaparambu, he was sent to the Vaikom English School. This suggests a rather progressive attitude on the part of his parents, both devout Muslims, since orthodox Kerala Muslims considered Malayalam and English to be languages of the kafirs. However, Basheer was taught Arabic at home by a musaliyar.

Those were the days of the freedom struggle. Young Basheer was excited when he first heard the names of Mahatma Gandhi, Jawaharlal Nehru, Maulana Abul Kalam Azad and others. A crucial moment in his life was when he literally "touched" Gandhiji during the latter's visit to Vaikom in March 1924 as part of the satyagraha movement. Gandhiji was demanding the right of entry to the Vaikom Temple for the lower castes.

by
M N Vijayan

When the reverberations of nationalist slogans reached Vaikom, Basheer, already inspired by Gandhiji, promptly responded by running away from home one night. Traversing long distances, he reached Ernakulam and boarded a train for Calicut in Malabar, the hub of nationalist activities. In a way, the nationalist movement turned out to be a momentous event in the literary history of Kerala as well.

Basheer joined the *Al-Amin* newspaper which was being managed by Muhammad Abdu Rahiman. Along with Rahiman and other activists, Basheer participated in the salt satyagraha on the Calicut beaches. Needless to say, he found himself in a lockup, from where he was sent to the Cannanore Central Jail.

Time and again, Basheer refers to the atrocities he was subjected to in police custody. By the time he was released, a dramatic change had come over him. Abandoning the Gandhian doctrine of ahimsa, he embraced terrorism as a means to curb the foreign power. Sardar Bhagat Singh, Raj Guru and Sukh Dev became his new role models. He moved to *Ujjevanam* (Revival), which became the mouthpiece of the terrorist movement, although it had been started as a Congress newspaper. As was expected, the police seized all subversive material, and *Ujjevanam* was banned. Basheer went underground, in order to avoid being arrested.

During the next seven years, Basheer travelled through the length and breadth of India, trying to elude the police. He drifted from one place to another, reaching the far shores of Arabia as well. In the course of his wanderings, he had to resort to various disguises and take on a variety of jobs. Basheer posed as a Hindu mendicant, a palmist, worked as a magician's assistant, a private tutor, a tea shop-keeper, to mention but a few of his strange occupations in the course of his travels.

In "Ormayute Arakal" (Chambers of Memory, 1973), he describes his attempt to join the film industry. He had gone to meet V Shantaram, the film director, wearing a rather outlandish outfit. Shantaram was in the process of shifting his studio from Kolhapur to Pune and promised to recruit him if Basheer managed to acquire even a smattering of Marathi.

Meanwhile, a beedi merchant named Gajanan came in contact with Basheer and was very impressed with his ability to converse fluently in Malayalam, English and Hindustani. At that time, Basheer was posing as an astrologer and Gajanan engaged him as a private tutor to teach English to his wards. Pleased with Basheer's competence, Gajanan wanted them to be taught arithmetic as well. But this was beyond Basheer's abilities. He left for Bombay after making some adequate excuse.

In Bombay, Basheer stayed for some time in Kamattipura, the notorious haunt of prostitutes, eunuchs and thieves. For a living, he worked in a shop crushing medicinal herbs for a vaidya. His fluency in English soon got him another job. He ran a night school in Bhindi Bazaar, teaching basic English, and earned five rupees a day.

Possessed by an intense desire to sail on the high seas, Basheer then joined as a khalasi on the *SS Rizvani*, which was taking Haj pilgrims from Bombay, through Aden along the Red Sea, to Jeddah. Though his desire to disembark at Jeddah and wander around Arabia did not materialize, he subsequently left the ship and headed for what is now Pakistan. Talking of the days he spent in Hyderabad (Sindh), Lahore and Peshawar, Basheer nostalgically remarks, "Why was India partitioned? A malicious act of the English when they knew they had to quit India. They injected poison into the minds of Hindus and Muslims. Pakistan is a wound on the shoulders of India."

While serving in a hotel in Karachi, Basheer heard of a vacancy in the *Civil and Military Gazette* where Rudyard Kipling had once worked. He was employed there as the proof reader's copy holder for a while. But soon he set out again and reached Delhi. During his stay in North India, Basheer visited practically all the sacred pilgrimages of the Hindus, Muslims and Christians. His wanderings took him to Ajmer, where he stayed in a dharmashala, posing as a Hindu. He also spent three-and-a-half years with sanyasis, practising meditation or dhyana. Then came a period with the Sufis, which was spent in chanting "Ya Ahad, Ya Ahad" through nights. Interacting with these religious sects was a fulfilling experience for Basheer whose inclination for the spiritual was as strong as his zest for worldly adventures.

Basheer next travelled to Peshawar and scaled the mountains that were inhabited by the ruthless Afridi tribe. After a brief sojourn there, he retraced his steps through what is now Pakistan to Kashmir where he met Sheikh Abdullah. His journey without maps, next led him to Calcutta. While trying his hand at various menial jobs, like washing vessels in hotels, he met a manufacturer of sports goods from Sialkot who offered him an agency in Kerala.

And Basheer finally returned home to find his father's business bankrupt and the family impoverished. He started working as an agent for the Sialkot sports company at Ernakulam. But he lost the agency when a bicycle accident incapacitated him temporarily.

On recovering, he resumed his endless hunt for jobs and found himself writing stories for a paper called *Jayakesari*. It was in this paper that his first story "Ente Thankam" (My Thankam) was published sometime between 1937 and 1941. A path breaker in Malayalam romantic fiction, it had as its heroine a dark-complexioned hunchback. This launched Basheer's career as a writer.

Meanwhile, articles directed at the undemocratic acts of the Dewan of Travancore brought Basheer under police surveillance again. And, unable to find sufficient outlets to vent his indignation, he started a weekly called *Pauranadam*, for which he wrote satirical stories as well. The weekly was banned and a warrant issued for his arrest. He lived in hiding with K C George, a prominent member of the newly formed Communist Party of Kerala. In the literary sphere, Basheer's friends at this point of time were Thakazhi Sivasankara Pillai, P C Kuttikrishnan, Changampuzha Krishna Pillai, Joseph Mundasseri and S K Pottekkat.

All this while, the police continued to harass Basheer's parents in order to get to him. A well-meaning police official suggested that the best course open to Basheer was to surrender to the police. He did so and served another term in prison. His experiences at the Kollam Kasba Police Station lockup are depicted in fictional form in stories like "Tiger" and "Itiyan Panikker." Free from rancour, these pungent satires exude genial humour, surprisingly. Another story about prison life is the romantic "Mathilukal" (Walls, 1965). While he was in prison he penned "Premalekhanam," a hilarious love story, requested by the numerous life prisoners who were on friendly terms with him. They had said to him, "Saare, we are fed up of reading the *Ramayana* and the *Bible*. Please write some stories for us."

Basheer's next spell as a writer and journalist was in Madras, where he contributed prolifically to the weekly *Jayakeralam*. Later, when he returned to Ernakulam, Basheer was involved in a variety of activities. He ran the Circle Book House which was later renamed Basheer's Book Stall. He also contributed a column called "The True and The False" to Raghavan Nair's *Narmada* which discussed every topic on the face of the earth, ranging from the most trivial to the most serious.

Prior to this, M P Paul, a respected teacher and literary critic, had advised him to pay more attention to his writing. It was Paul who really launched him as a writer with his insightful and encouraging criticism of *Balyakalasakhi* (Childhood Friend, 1944), a simple and poignant story of unfulfilled love.

The book stall had to be wound up when Basheer had a nervous breakdown for which he had to be treated for six years. He has spoken most uninhibitedly about it. "Many years ago I suffered from acute insanity. Although prolonged treatment has cured it, one can see vestiges of it in the many things I have said and written." The novella, *Pathummayute Adu* (Pathumma's Goat, 1959) was written, he says, while undergoing treatment.

In 1958, persuaded by friends, Basheer married Fatima Bi. They shifted to Beypore in 1962. He lived there till his death on July 5, 1994. The last three decades of Basheer's life were marked by what may be called a writer's block. In frail health, seated under the shade of his favourite mangosteen tree, he passed his time listening to ghazals and talking to a never-ending stream of visitors. While the superannuated Basheer has been made into a cult figure, the man behind his writings was the restless soul frenziedly wandering in pursuit of experience.

Background information may seem irrelevant when discussing a writer's work, but in Basheer's case it is not so. A gripping raconteur, he turned to account all his experiences when he began writing. Politics and prison, asceticism, pickpocketing, homosexuality, all were grist to his mill. The private and the public, the world of action and the world of imagination, coalesced when Basheer wrote fiction and quasi-fiction. His wide travels symbolize his journeys to the different regions of human experience as well. Between the sublime "Anal Huq" or "Aham Brahmasmi" and the infernal Kamattipura, we have a host of other experiences drawn from the mundane everyday existence of human beings. Whether it be the crook or the nitwit, the wicked or the innocent, the "I" of his tales gazes at "god's plenty" spread out before him and presents this to us, distilled in the alembic of his rich humour.

It was in the early 1930s that the first impact of what is called "Jeevatasahityam" or progressive writing was felt in the sphere of Malayalam literature. It is important for the reader of Basheer's stories to keep in mind his picaresque life against the backdrop of the literary scenario of Malayalam fiction in the 1930s.

Basheer was a contemporary of reputed fiction writers like Karur Nilakanta Pillai (1858-1975), Kesav Dev (1904-83), Ponkunnam Varki (1908-), Lalithambika Antharjanam (1909-87), Thakazhi Sivasankara Pillai (1912-), S K Pottekkat (1913-82) and P C Kuttikrishnan "Uroob" (1915-79). Basheer shares with these writers only a certain social conjuncture and consciousness. Dev, Varki and Thakazhi were the first conscious practitioners of socialist writing. They imaginatively rendered into words their vicarious experience of poverty and the sordidness accompanying it, while Basheer objectively recorded his personal experience of penury.

Though he shares with S K Pottekkat the experience of extensive travelling, it is only Basheer who transforms journeys into literary experiences. If he is the master of the colloquial style it is because of the exigencies of his circumstances. He forged his own style and told his own stories, most of them disguised as autobiography, and unwittingly became the first Muslim fiction writer in Kerala to challenge the prevalent literary conventions of sanskritized Malayalam.

Basheer's ignorance of literary conventions, and the lack of the homogenizing social background that had moulded the writings of his contemporaries, combined with a native talent for narration, made him the unique writer that he was. As he himself says, "agonizing experiences and a pen" were all that he had when he set out to write fiction. He initially wrote "potboilers," literally to ward off pangs of hunger. He speaks of his early struggles as a writer in his foreword to *Visappu* (Hunger, 1954). They are also well depicted in *Kathabeejam* The Germ of a Story, 1945), the only play he wrote.

As a young man, I first knew Basheer in 1945. By that time, *Balyakalasakhi* had been published, earning him fame as a writer. But it was not in the pages of a book or in the critical columns that I saw him. I remember him as the owner of a small book stall in a crowded Ernakulam jetty, seated on a rickety folding chair, touting a few books stacked on a shelf fixed to the wall.

The Second World War had been drawing to a close, I remember. The issues that invaded young minds were rooted in their immediate environment. Issues like poverty, unemployment, death and senseless destruction. Basheer's seminal work, "Sabdangal" (Voices, 1947), reflects all of these crucial issues and is the microcosm of the very world we live in. This work may be considered a precursor of modern fiction in Kerala. With the eye of a camera, the narrator focuses on montage-like scenes from where emanate a rabble of voices – stark and staccato, the terseness a characteristic feature of Basheer's style.

What Basheer brought to Malayalam writing is a new way of looking at human lives. Set against the backdrop of social conventions and literary traditions drawn on sanskritized Malayalam, Basheer's writing is really a mirror of the contemporary Indian experience. Through a humour directed at an awkward nose, a bald head or an excessively romantic temperament, he has taught us the rare language of irony.

In the trilogy – *Balyakalasakhi, N'te Uppooppakkoru Anadarnu* and *Pathummayute Adu* – Basheer portrays the Kerala Muslim ethos. But the experiences he deals with in his innumerable other shorter writings are not confined to a particular community or locale. His area is the human community and all the issues are universal. This is what singles him out from his contemporaries. By addressing the concerns of the present generation, he reveals his modern sensibility as no other writer of his period has done. In "Anarghanimisham" (The Invaluable Moment) and "Sandhyapranamam" (An Evening Prayer), for instance, the angst of the modern man is articulated. Whereas "Bhoomiyute Avakasikal" (The Rightful Inheritors of the Earth) is concerned with preserving the ecological balance in a world dominated by human beings. Rearing a garden wherever he was, whether in jail or at home, was an absorbing interest of his. He loved music as much as he loved flowers.

In Basheer, there seems to be no rift between the man and the writer. He often said that he became a writer only because he lacked the training required to be a cook, a magician, a coconut-palm climber, a journalist or a pickpocket. In his view there is nothing great or profound about Literature. He has shown us how card-sharpers, prostitutes, holy men, all create languages which articulate their experiences, there being no difference between these languages and the so-called language of Literature.

In a career that spanned thirty years, Basheer did not publish very much. Whether the absence of a continuous stream of creative writing

should be construed as a writer's lack or a comment on his imaginative
vigour is an open question. Some critics do express dissatisfaction
with the brevity of most of his fictional works. The writer's answer to
them is that utmost economy is one of his stylistic dicta.

The skill of Basheer's narrative technique seems to exceed that of
most of his contemporaries. With great ease, he plunges the reader
into the various labyrinths of an experience. This accounts for the
variety in his narrative strategies. No two stories of his are alike. The
lands traversed by Basheer, the peaks of experience he scaled, the
abysmal depths he plunged into, cannot fail to amaze any reader.
What is even more astonishing is the manner in which he transformed
all these experiences into the stories he tells us, converting the
biographical into the historical, the transient into the perennial and
the trivial into the sublime.

Tellicherry
August 1996

The card-sharper's daughter

The moral of this story may as well be delivered right at the beginning. Girls will find it neither amusing nor enlightening. Anyway, here it is. If you happen to have daughters, steel your heart and murder them all in cold blood!

Now don't think that these are my views. I earnestly hope and pray that none of the many honourable ladies among my readers, incensed by this blatantly misogynist observation, condemns me to eternal damnation. They should target Ottakkannan Pokker instead!

Ottakkannan Pokker is the tragic protagonist of this story. Mandan Muthapa may be loosely described as the villain, though, as the story progresses, he steadily rises in stature to become the hero, the chivalrous knight who takes up arms against Pokker. Zainaba is Muthapa's comrade-in-arms in the battle.

The constables of the village outpost, both stooges of the tyrannical regime, and Thorappan Avaran and Driver Pappunni, the two master rogues, were out of station. Anavari Raman Nair and Ponkurissu Thoma, bigwigs of the local criminal fraternity, were holding the fort for them. Ettukali Mammoonhu, their protége, was always at hand. So were the other villagers, who were more than twenty-two hundred in number. All of them were peace-lovers, they had nothing to do with warmongering reactionaries.

These are the essential facts which I, as a humble chronicler, would like my readers to acquaint themselves

translated by
K M Sherrif

with. Apart from these, it would be prudent to note the presence of a floating population of about twenty-six hundred men and women who appeared only on Tuesdays and Saturdays, the village market-days. Their role was confined to buying and selling and making a great ruckus – with a few scuffles thrown in. Ottakkannan Pokker and Mandan Muthapa were artists who rubbed shoulders with this multitude as they pursued their respective vocations. Zainaba also belonged to the ranks of the people, though she was seldom seen in their midst. Her creative endeavours were shrouded in mystery.

Would you ever trust your daughters if you knew what they were up to? Why do they cause the best-laid schemes of their fathers to go awry? What do daughters know of the agonies of a father's heart!

I must confess that, after interviewing the major characters of the story, I felt a certain partiality towards some of them and consequently lent them my moral support. I record here the whole story for the benefit of students of history.

I shall begin with Ottakkannan Pokker. As the sobriquet prefixed to his name indicates, he had only one eye. It had been damaged beyond repair in one of the heroic adventures of his salad days. It was true that certain intellectuals in the locality surreptitiously referred to him as "that one-eyed monkey." But never mind that. When this story begins, he was forty-nine years old. His complexion could be described as fair. The real colour of his teeth was a well-concealed secret. The visible colour was a dull red, owing to the fact that Pokker was a voracious betel-chewer. And by virtue of his profession, "Ottakkannan Pokker, the card-sharper" was how he was popularly referred to.

I suppose you have deduced from what has already been said that Zainaba was Pokker's daughter. Nineteen years of age, she was the village beauty. She had to be married off to some hard-working young man. This was what drove Ottakkannan Pokker to work tirelessly, day in and day out.

Pokker had already accumulated a sum of one hundred and twenty rupees towards this end. Now, what happened to this money? Zainaba didn't steal it. Anavari, Ponkurissu, Thorappan, Ettukali and their admirers were all innocent of the crime though, as a rule, the institution of private property was anathema to them. The two constables had nothing to do with it either. Mandan Muthapa? Certainly not! The fact is, nobody stole it. What happened to it then? Wait, I am coming to that.

The focus of the narrative now shifts to Mandan Muthapa, a young man of twenty-one, jet-black in complexion and slightly cross-eyed. However, he always had a charming smile on his face. Like Zainaba, he had lost his mother in his childhood. His father had died a martyr's death in prison after a pitched battle with a bunch of beastly policemen over some misunderstanding about a burglary. As far as he could remember, he did not have any kith or kin. People just called him "Mandan Muthapa, the pickpocket."

"Mandan" or "nitwit" had been prefixed to Muthapa's name by none other than Pokker. In a way, Pokker was Muthapa's mentor, having taught him the technique of exhaling smoke through one's nose. Though Muthapa was required to pay a fee of one rupee for the lesson, he had unbelted only five-and-a-half annas. The loss still rankled. "That bastard Mandan owes me ten-and-a-half annas," Pokker would wrathfully say, "I taught him to blow smoke through his nose." This claim dealt a crushing blow to Muthapa's ambitions. Muthapa had just begun his career as an apprentice to Anavari Raman Nair and Ponkurissu Thoma. Pokker's statement prompted these gentlemen to have second thoughts about their young apprentice,

---

Ottakkannan: One-eyed. **Mandan:** Slow-witted. **Anavari:** Elephant-stealer. **Ponkurissu:** Golden Cross. **Thorappan:** Mole. **Ettukali:** Spider.

All these characters feature in several stories and novellas of Basheer, which he describes as "the records of a humble chronicler." Detailed accounts of their exploits can be found in *Anavariyum Ponkurissum, Sthalathe Pradhana Divyan* and *Oru Bhagavad Gitayum Kure Mulakalum.*

and Muthapa was left to fend for himself in a wicked world. Who would employ a Mandan – a dunce – when bright young boys jostled for attention?

Before he started picking pockets, Mandan Muthapa had tried to enroll himself as Pokker's pupil in card-sharping. He had managed to get his case recommended by a few influential well-wishers as well. But Pokker had refused to oblige. "Get lost, you donkey. It needs boys with brains to do this stuff."

Pokker was right there. Brains were an asset in any profession and card-sharping demanded an exceptionally high level of intelligence – and, of course, capital. Pokker had both. His kit consisted of a pack of cards, an old issue of *Malayala Manorama* and a handful of small stones. The stones served as paperweights when the musty newspaper was spread out and the pack of cards placed on it. Shuffling the cards briskly, Pokker would take out three from the pack, one joker and two numbered cards. The next step was to exhibit these cards face-up for his clients to take a good look at them, the joker in one hand and the numbered cards in the other. But some vigorous sales-talk was necessary before the clients could be won over completely. So Pokker would clear his throat and unleash his oratorical skills on them. "Hai raja ... come on everybody ... double your money, folks ... two for one, four for two, the joker makes your fortune. Never mind if you place your money on the numbered cards. It's your alms for a poor man ... hai raja ..."

Pokker would flick the cards facedown on the paper with a whirring motion. It was the gamblers' responsibility to observe the movement of the cards carefully. Hawk-eyed, they would stare before placing their bets on the cards of their choice. Most of them placed anna coins and one-rupee notes on the cards, though there were also some who wagered as much as five or ten rupees. But when the cards were turned, they would find that the joker had eluded them – as always. Thus, each round ended with defeat for the valiant people and success for the wily Pokker. He would calmly scoop up the money, of which two rupees went to the local constabulary.

But it was not amusing to play to lose all the time. So Pokker hit upon a brilliant strategy. On an average, the people won nearly six times out of ten. Amazing! But, there was a catch. For "people," read "friends and apprentices of Pokker whose identities were unknown to the market crowd." There was no fraud in this really!

Yet what a world of difference there was between Ottakkannan Pokker's and Mandan Muthapa's professions! Contrary to popular opinion, there is nothing demeaning about a pickpocket's work. It has made amazing strides in many countries of the world. There are even colleges to train aspiring pickpockets. That apart, it is a profession which requires unwavering concentration, infinite patience, an eye for detail and unshaken faith in the adage "silence is golden." And, as I have already mentioned, some brains would certainly help. Did Mandan Muthapa have any brains? Well ... grit and determination will see the professional pickpocket through many a crisis.

As for capital, long nimble fingers and a shawl are the only tools required. Like all committed artists, a pickpocket has to have a finger on the pulse of the people. Not for him the solitary existence of the ivory tower. In other words, a pickpocket is essentially a social being, sharing the joys and sorrows of the people. "Community living" is the pickpocket's motto. Weddings, funerals, cattle-trading posts, carnivals, processions, wrestling matches, political meetings – wherever human beings congregate – he presents himself to unburden the unwary of their filthy lucre.

The modus operandi is simple. Single out a man from the crowd who looks well-to-do, cover his pocket with the shawl and, with a quick movement of the long fingers, deftly remove the wallet or pouch. Speed is of the essence and it can be achieved only through sustained practice. But that is not all. The loot has to be passed on to an apprentice who immediately effects a vanishing trick.

Unfortunately, of all the requirements listed above, a shawl and long nimble fingers were all that Muthapa possessed. His height of six feet and two inches was a liability. He was a full head taller than most men in the crowd that thronged the village on market-days. No sooner did he appear on the scene than there would be a cry from the crowd, "Hey you, be careful! Mandan Muthapa has taken a liking to you." A typical instance of the scant respect society gives to artists!

However, none of these zealots belonged to the village. They were all outsiders, henchmen of the hated establishment. They had closed their ranks against Mandan Muthapa. Unlike the workers of certain political parties, Muthapa did not let out hoarse-throated slogans, condemning his detractors for being "bourgeois reactionaries." He merely flashed his charming, innocent smile that mesmerized them and unsuspecting bystanders alike. But not the village constables. They squeezed Muthapa to the tune of one rupee each market-day. The politically-conscious villagers had no use for these representatives of the powers that be and opposed this high-handedness. But that made no difference to the constables who were determined to have their cut of Muthapa's earnings. How could Muthapa manage when, in spite of his toils, he earned next to nothing on several days? To make matters worse, Ottakkannan Pokker was always at hand to give prosecution evidence against Muthapa. "That bastard Mandan cleaned up ten rupees today. I saw the racket with my own eyes."

"You one-eyed devil!" Mandan Muthapa would mutter, "I'll gouge out your good eye one of these days."

The equation was now clear and known to one and all. The arch-enemies had taken to the battlefield. Mandan Muthapa, the pickpocket, universally acknowledged to be a nitwit, and Ottakkannan Pokker, the card-sharper, whose wits never deserted him. The tale which I am about to unfold before you describes how Mandan Muthapa, the nitwit, vanquished his nimble-witted adversary and won the hand of … well, I should not kill the suspense. Let me begin at the beginning.

It was a Saturday. Ottakkannan Pokker had presented himself under the ancient silk-cotton tree in the marketplace well before the clamour of the market-day had begun. Mandan Muthapa, having had no breakfast, was feeling rather down in the dumps that morning. There were no good samaritans around to buy him even a cup of tea. But as he came down the lane, hungry and dejected, there appeared before him a man in a long jubba. This man wore a gold-plated wristwatch and had an expensive looking fountain pen clipped to the pocket of his jubba. Muthapa's heart skipped a beat. As the man walked on jauntily with the air of a millionaire, oblivious of his surroundings, puffing at a cigarette, Muthapa relieved him of his wallet.

It was one of the most successful jobs Muthapa had pulled off. But the contents of the wallet did not delight him. Five-and-a-half annas and the photograph of a film actress who wore a nose-stud were all that he got for his pains. "Damn her nose-stud!" Muthapa cursed, tearing the photograph into bits. "Him and his almighty airs! The miser!"

The newly-opened restaurant was doing brisk business. Muthapa decided to give it a try. He seated himself next to a fat man whose side-pocket looked promising. But nothing came of it. Muthapa quietly finished the snacks and tea the waiter had served him unsolicited. It came to four annas. He bought beedis for half-an-anna, and with the remaining capital of one anna, presented himself before Ottakkannan Pokker.

"Hai raja ... come on ... two for one ... any mandan ass can try ..." Ottakkannan Pokker said, before throwing the cards facedown on a sheet of paper. Muthapa placed the anna on what he judged to be the joker. "Get lost, you ass," Pokker told him gently as he turned the card. It was a numbered card.

"Would you like another try?" Pokker asked with a mocking wink.

Muthapa had run out of money. Lighting a beedi, he walked away from the crowd, towards the solitude of the river. How sad is the plight of a poor artist! How agonizing it is to think of what might have been! In his heart, Mandan Muthapa worshipped Thorappan Avaran, Driver Pappunni, Ponkurissu Thoma and Anavari Raman Nair as his mentors. If only they would accept him as their pupil. That Ottakkannan Pokker, curse him! He had spoilt everything.

Lost in thought, Muthapa walked on. His steps took him down the path by the river. The market landing was crowded with boats. There were large mounds of tapioca, coconuts, bananas and a variety of vegetables all around. As he gazed listlessly at the boats loaded with merchandise, Muthapa witnessed a miracle!

A bunch of bananas dragged itself out of a mound, climbed over the side of the boat and leaped into the river! It was not one of those accidents when things topple into the river from overloaded boats. The bunch of bananas did it slowly, deliberately – as if it were alive!

This set Muthapa thinking. Were the bananas possessed by a devil? he wondered. Consigned to the plant kingdom by nature, they would certainly require a devil's services to "walk away" as they had. They were now moving steadily in the water towards the next landing where Ottakkannan Pokker lived. A row of silk-cotton trees, that stretched between the two landings, functioned as a wide curtain.

His curiosity aroused, Muthapa walked towards the landing downstream, following the bananas with his eyes. Suddenly, startling him, appeared Zainaba, Pokker's only daughter. Crouching in the shadow of the trees, she was pulling at a strong string that stretched towards the river. Soon she pulled up the bunch of bananas which had reached its destination. There was a fishing hook attached to the bunch, Muthapa noted.

In a flash, everything fell into place, like the pieces of a jigsaw puzzle. It was a simple process. Swim down to the market landing under cover of the bushes with a hook attached to a long line. Fix the hook to a bunch of bananas and swim back downstream, unwinding the line gently. Hide behind the clump of silk-cotton trees, pull the bananas, and they are yours.

Mandan Muthapa was distressed. There was nothing wrong in men stealing or picking pockets. But for a woman to do so ... He stood transfixed, afflicted by Zainaba's indiscretion.

Zainaba climbed ashore with the bunch of bananas, water dripping from her wet clothes. She had no inkling of Muthapa's presence. When her eyes fell on him, she dropped the bananas with a gasp. Her face turned a deep purple, and then white as chalk.

"Zainaba!" There was love and anguish in Muthapa's voice.

"O!" Zainaba answered in a broken voice.

"Do you think what you have done is right?"

"Nnnno ..."

"Will you do it again?"

"No."

"Change your clothes and wipe yourself dry. You will catch a cold."

Zainaba ran, without taking the bananas. Muthapa carried them home for her. She had a small restaurant there. Besides tea, it served puttu, boiled black gram, appam, vada and bananas. She gave credit to some of her regular customers, among whom were Anavari Raman Nair, Ponkurissu Thoma and Ettukali Mammoonhu. When they reached her house, she invited Muthapa in for tea with idiyappam and bananas.

Muthapa testifies to all these facts. Zainaba, however, refused to reply when she was confronted by this chronicler and asked whether she loved Muthapa. But she was quite certain that Muthapa was not a mandan. "Bapa says that out of spite," she said.

Ottakkannan Pokker was completely ignorant of all this. He was not suspicious of Zainaba. Preoccupied with the task of putting by some money for her wedding, he did not notice such things. An honest and hard-working boy had to be found. She should have a few pairs of earrings and necklaces for the wedding. These were his concerns.

That day, Pokker was returning home with a bag of provisions he had bought at the market. The first sight that greeted his eyes when he stepped into the house was that of Mandan Muthapa, his head reclining in Zainaba's lap.

What more was required to break a poor father's heart? A dark, cross-eyed, stupid pickpocket nestling in your daughter's lap! One rarely comes across a father who would find it funny.

"Bapa!" Zainaba leapt up in terror as she pushed Muthapa away. But Mandan Muthapa merely flashed his charming smile.

Ottakkannan Pokker was furious. He flung a piece of tapioca at Muthapa which struck him square on his chest. Though it hurt him considerably, Muthapa, without removing the smile from his face, picked it up, peeled it gently and nibbled at it. "Mama, you know I am going to marry Zainaba," he said.

Now this was a double-edged statement. Firstly, "mama" is a term used to address one's maternal uncle or wife's father. As we know, neither of these relationships existed between Ottakkannan Pokker and Mandan Muthapa. Was Muthapa taking a leap into the future? Besides, as you might have noticed, Muthapa's statement was a bold assertion, not a humble request like "May I beg for the hand of your fair daughter" etcetera.

Ottakkannan Pokker shook with rage. "Get out of my house, you thieving scoundrel!" he screamed.

"Mama, forgive me for all I have said and done to you. Zainaba says I should stop picking pockets. So I'm not going to any more."

"I see. You are taking to begging instead."

"I want to set up a small restaurant," Muthapa continued, ignoring the sarcasm. "Mama, will you lend me ten rupees for it?"

"What about the ten-and-a-half annas you owe me for teaching you to smoke through the nose?"

Mandan Muthapa ignored that too. "Any day before the end of the month would suit me for the wedding."

"Get out, you blasted Jew!" Ottakkannan Pokker roared. "Don't get any such ideas as long as I am alive."

But the veiled threat did not deter Muthapa. "Mama, I'll marry Zainaba long before you die."

Jew: Used here as a term of abuse. Like Pokker, Muthapa too was a Muslim.

"Get out!"

Mandan Muthapa walked away calmly.

This was the beginning of a long struggle, a fight to the finish. The news spread like wildfire. The villagers were merely amused at first. But soon they split into opposing camps. In the beginning, the two constables were staunch supporters of Ottakkannan Pokker. But soon they, along with the vast majority of the villagers, shifted their loyalties to Mandan Muthapa. There was a good reason for such a move. But more about it later.

Where did Zainaba's loyalties lie? the villagers wondered.

"Zainaba's with me," declared Mandan Muthapa, drawing himself to his full height and thumping his chest.

"She's my daughter," Ottakkannan Pokker said with some amount of confidence.

But the fact was that nobody really knew anything about Zainaba's loyalties. Meanwhile, Anavari Raman Nair and Ponkurissu Thoma made a joint statement, "It is a battle for Zainaba's heart."

To the villagers, this sounded like one of the most stupid things they had ever heard. Did the duo really believe that the union of two hearts was all that mattered? There was an obstinate father to be reckoned with. That and the hundred and twenty rupees, his life's earnings. Ottakkannan Pokker was in a position to marry Zainaba to any young man of his choice. This was the state of affairs when Muthapa declared war.

Right from the beginning, Mandan Muthapa's offensive met with remarkable success. He was the universally acclaimed leader of the masses.

Pokker was denounced as a hoarder, a black-marketeer, and above all, a bourgeois reactionary.

"Mandan Muthapa zindabad!"

"Ottakkannan Pokker murdabad!"

Slogans rent the air. There was no dearth of people to buy tea and lunch for Muthapa whenever he needed them. On the other hand, Pokker found it difficult to get even a pinch of slaked lime for his betel-and-nut.

It was a Tuesday. The marketplace was beginning to bustle with buyers and sellers. Mandan Muthapa appeared without his customary shawl. He held a one-rupee note in his hand. He had pinched it with his teeth. "This is a lucky note," he was heard telling a man in the crowd, "Zainaba gave it to me."

Muthapa headed straight for Ottakkannan Pokker's gambling corner. As usual, a small crowd had collected in front of it.

"Hai raja, come on. Double your money. The joker is your lucky boy. Keep your eyes peeled. Hai raja ..."

Mandan Muthapa clutched the one-rupee note between his thumb and forefinger and sniffed at it rather noisily. Ottakkannan Pokker looked up at Muthapa and continued with his sales-talk, inserting a couple of unusual expressions in between. "Hai raja, double your money. Any sucker can try his luck, any stuffed monkey can try his luck. The joker is your lucky boy ..."

Pokker flicked the cards facedown on the paper. Mandan Muthapa scrutinized the cards carefully and placed his one-rupee note on one of them. Pokker winced as if he had been pricked with a pin. In twenty-two years of card-sharping, nobody had placed his money on the joker without Pokker's express permission. Perhaps a handful of lucky chaps had got the card right purely by accident. Their number was, however, too small for Pokker to remember. There was absolutely no connection between card-sharping and luck. The golden rule was that Pokker should always win and the market-day crowd lose.

Ottakkannan Pokker turned the cards. There was a gasp from the crowd. Muthapa's one-rupee note had been on the joker. And Pokker grudgingly gave him another rupee.

"Hai raja, two for one, four for two ... open to all and sundry ..." The game resumed.

As before, Mandan Muthapa looked carefully at each card before placing his two rupees on one of them. Ottakkannan Pokker turned the cards. The joker again for Muthapa! He now had four rupees.

When Muthapa's luck persisted in the next round, Pokker lost his temper. The crowd let out a whoop of joy.

Muthapa's luck held out. He gazed at the windfall in his hand – sixteen rupees – and rustled the notes gently. He took out the one-rupee note, which had been his capital when he started, kissed it reverentially and tied it at the end of his mundu. He then announced his future plans to the crowd, "I am through with picking pockets. I am going to set up a tea shop."

Mandan Muthapa walked away triumphantly, accompanied by his fellow artists – Anavari Raman Nair, Ponkurissu Thoma and Ettukali Mammoonhu. Behind them came a host of villagers, their spirit for battle aroused. Soon the whole village learned of Muthapa's triumph. There was universal rejoicing. It was a victory for the people!

There was not a soul to commiserate with the vanquished Pokker. But then, one can't expect people to sympathize with black-marketeers and lackeys of reactionary regimes.

"Daughter, I lost fifteen rupees today," Pokker told Zainaba mournfully that night. "That scoundrel did me in."

She said nothing. There was neither sympathy nor exhilaration in her expression. But Pokker's grief knew no bounds. "I am not finished," he said, regaining his composure, "Let that Mandan have another try. I'll skin him. Pokker doesn't take things lying down."

Come market-day, the hawkers arrived with their wares. Men and women jostled as they sought to make their bargains. Muthapa's tea shop had opened just a few days before. As a matter of fact, no tea was served there. Only coffee with jaggery, and boiled gram to go with it. It was an apology for a tea shop, functioning in the open space between two buildings, sheets of cloth hung up on poles to make an enclosure. An old bench, the only item of furniture, and two glasses to serve coffee in. Noisily stirring the jaggery in a glass with a spoon, he invited his customers, "Hai, Mandan's coffee! Sizzling hot! Have a sip folks, gives you more than your money's worth."

The coffee and the boiled black gram were sold out before noon. Muthapa counted his earnings and wrapped the notes and coins in a piece of paper. With this packet, he presented himself before Pokker.

Ottakkannan Pokker lost twenty rupees that day. When he told Zainaba about it that night, she merely shrugged her shoulders. "Oh, I suppose everybody has caught on to the trick by now."

"Caught on! Listen, you stupid ... Nobody caught on to it in the last twenty-two years. You mean to say that bastard Mandan did it in a couple of days?"

Zainaba said nothing.

"I taught that stingy Jew how to blow out smoke through his nose!"

A dozen market-days passed by. Mandan Muthapa continued to subject Ottakkannan Pokker to humiliating defeats. Pokker was now at the end of his tether, broke and neck-deep in debt. And finally, he admitted defeat. "Son, leave me alone, please," he pleaded with Muthapa. "I'll give you five rupees on each market-day."

"I don't want your money," said the long-suffering Muthapa. "I have my shop now. Let me marry Zainaba, and I'll quit card-sharping for good."

Marriage to Zainaba – Muthapa was firm on this compromise formula. So were the valiant villagers.

Ottakkannan Pokker ran from pillar to post for help. He beseeched the two constables to come to his aid. He unburdened his heart to Anavari Raman Nair, Ponkurissu Thoma and Ettukali Mammoonhu. But his pleas fell on deaf ears. "Get Zainaba married to that fellow, man," they told him in one voice.

"But, my dear sir, he is a mandan."

"There you go again!"
Pokker was left with no option.

The whole village attended the wedding. Muthapa treated them to betel-nut, beedis and sherbet. At night, there was a display of fireworks sponsored by the villagers.

It was a happy ending to a long conflict. But not quite. Ottakkannan Pokker was heartbroken. He quit card-sharping. He lost his appetite and always wore a melancholy expression on his face. He hated everyone – Zainaba, Anavari Raman Nair, Ponkurissu Thoma, the constables, Ettukali Mammoonhu, and the decadent social order which sustained them. Pokker stopped eating altogether, determined to fast unto death.

The kindhearted villagers intervened. After a lot of cajoling, they succeeded in persuading Pokker to live with Zainaba and Muthapa in the annexe to their hotel. Yes, the make-shift tea shop had graduated into a proper hotel! Zainaba's puttu and boiled black gram were in great demand.

The enterprise was wholeheartedly supported by Zainaba's regular customers – Anavari Raman Nair, Ponkurissu Thoma, their protégé Ettukali Mammoonhu, and the two constables. Like them, Pokker could eat his fill and he was required to do no work.

But there was something which tormented Pokker like a thorn in his flesh. How could Mandan Muthapa place his money unfailingly on the joker all the time? Unable to bear it any longer, he put the question to Muthapa himself.

"Just brains," Muthapa replied, tapping his forehead.

Pokker knew it was too good to be true. Where could Mandan Muthapa get brains from, he who was willing to *part* with precious money for learning to let out smoke through the nose?

When Pokker persisted, Muthapa revealed the secret. "It was my wife's brain wave."

Zainaba's brain wave! Mandan Muthapa produced the evidence. The corners of all the jokers in the pack had been marked out by small holes made with a safety pin!

"What do you think, son?" Ottakkannan Pokker asked me, "Can you ever trust your daughters?"

Well, what can one say ...!

This story was first published as "Mucheettukalikkarante Makal" in 1951.

Walls

Have you heard a little love story called "Walls?" I don't think I have narrated it ever before. I had thought of calling it "A Woman's Fragrance" or "The Scent of a Woman" or some such thing. You know how we talk of Fate, Time and things like that. Well, this incident comes from the far side of that great Time – only, I am on this side now, a lonely heart. This is a song of grief from the vast shores of that heart.

High stone walls that seem to touch the sky, circle me. There are several buildings within the boundary of the Central Jail. And numerous people. All the prisoners have been locked up. No particular sounds can be heard. Some prisoners are to be hanged at dawn. Some have completed their terms and will be released into the world of freedom tomorrow. Yet, a sort of calm prevails.

We are walking. Somewhat close to the gallows. On a very narrow path. All around us, stretching into the distance, are the walls. Ahead of me walks the warder. It has been only minutes since they put me into prison clothes and transformed me into a number. A white cap striped in black, a white shirt, white mundu. A rug to sleep on, a blanket to cover myself with, dishes to eat and drink from ... Each one of these is numbered. I am not new to all this. Several times have I been in jail and become a number.

translated by
Nivedita Menon

Long ago I had read a book called *Numerology*. Remembering it, I looked at my new number. Added the digits. Nine. Good. What is the significance of nine? What will I go through in this jail? My thoughts wandered. My pace slackened.

"Walk a little faster, can't you?" the warder ordered. That made me laugh. I never waste an opportunity to laugh. God's greatest gift to humanity – laughter.

I asked, "Where are you off to in such a hurry ... are you off from this earth itself?"

The warder was silent. He kept walking. I said, "I suppose you have to rush off to some important business after you have locked me up?"

The charge against me *was* a little serious. Some reserve policemen had threatened to crush my right hand into cotton-fluff, from the tip of the middle finger to my shoulder. Of course, my parents, brothers and sisters were not actually informed by the police. They were told by the magistrate – the cheek of the police! And then the police had laid siege on my house. To arrest me. I was not there. I was caught later. But no one beat me. I was put into a major police lockup in a town some fifty-sixty miles away. For fourteen months or so, the case did not come up for a hearing. I was just locked up! Following the advice of a police inspector, I made an issue of it. I fasted. That is, I went on a hunger strike, a satyagraha! Which is how I managed to get the case to court and was awarded a sentence.

In the lockup, I had spent my days as a member of the family, under the benevolent gaze of a few hundred constables and inspectors. Many of them had become my disciples. I had the status of a head constable there. I also wrote several police stories during my stay in the lockup. The Inspector had provided me with paper and pencils. I bid farewell to everyone and set out, escorted by two policemen carrying guns and handcuffs. They brought me here, to the Central Jail. But all this is besides the point.

The two policemen had given me two packets of beedis, matches and a brand-new blade. With the grand announcement that, "This kind of thing is forbidden in jail," this warder took it all away. He removed his high headgear, put my things into it, covered them with a piece of old cloth, and replaced it on his head. And now, there he was, walking along as if nothing had happened. Let him. The beast!

What was the blade for, you ask. Nothing that you could possibly imagine. One can split a match stick into four with it. Why, these eyes have seen artists who have split one match into six. It is not easy to come by matches in the jail. After all, that requires money. And money is something one does not have. At such times, the blade can be quite a useful little implement. Not all by itself, but to make what I call a chakki. This is how the chakki is born. From the rug provided by the government, pull out some threads, each as long as your palm, till you have them to a thickness of two fingers. Tie the threads together, leaving a head of two inches or so. Set fire to this head and burn it well. What true artists do is to wrap up the burnt ends in a piece of leather folded several times. But poor people like me have to make do with the thick leaf of a jackfruit.

Now if you have a small piece of steel, you can rub it on cement or stone at any time to produce a spark. You can introduce this spark to the charred ends of the chakki, and there it is – fire! But where would one get steel? Almost everything else is, of course, available in the jail – not just wax but beedis, matches, ganja, booze, jaggery. If you have the money. But if you have a blade, you have steel! You must preserve the blade by pushing it deep into a piece of wood. Such were the marvels secreted away in the noble warder's cap!

I remarked, "Policemen are not bad!"

Hadn't he heard? He walked on silently. He would sell anything for a profit. The so-and-so must have made enough to feed his children and his grandchildren and even get the moon and the stars for them.

I asked him, "How many children do you have?"

Awakened from his musings, he replied, "Six. Five girls and a boy."

Poor warder! Five girls!

"And are the children and their mother well?"

"Yes, yes," he said, impatiently. "Walk faster."

The reason for his hurry was suddenly clear to me.

"What will happen to them if you die?" I asked then.

"God will provide for them."

"I doubt that."

The warder asked, "Why?"

"Divine knowledge!" I replied. "I was a sanyasi once. There is not a single holy mosque or temple in India that I haven't visited. Not one sacred river I haven't bathed in. Mountain peaks, valleys, forests, deserts, seacoasts, ruined temples ..."

"So what?"

"God will not leave you unpunished!"

"But I haven't done anything wrong."

"What about the daylight robbery you committed today?"

He seemed surprised. "What robbery?"

"One day, you die and your soul appears before the divine presence. God asks then, Oh you wretched jail-warder, where are the matches, the blade and the two packets of beedis you took from poor Basheer?"

The warder stood silent and still. "Come, come. Don't you have to rush off to your business after locking me up?" I asked.

He did not move. Then, shaking with silent laughter, he removed his cap and returned my treasures.

"Good fellow!" I said. "The Inspector told me this morning that Gandhiji is on a fast. Have you heard anything about it?"

He replied, "He has ended his fast by drinking lime juice." Good. Mohandas Karamchand Gandhi zindabad! Zindabad, all humanity!

We walked on, passing many iron doors. Walls! Walls!

"How many political prisoners does this jail have?"

"There are seventeen where you are going to be kept. Counting you, there would be eighteen."

So, we were going to a special place. The government was taking this fellow seriously! Good.

As we walked on, I was overcome by the most maddening scent in the world. The scent of a woman! Female fragrance!

I was shaken. Every little atom of my being was aroused. My nostrils expanded. I inhaled and drew into myself ... everything in this world.

Where was she? I looked around. Nobody! Nothing!

And as we continued, my ears heard the most beautiful sound in the world. A woman's laughter!

Had this sound and this fragrance come together? Or had I imagined one in the wake of the other?

I had almost forgotten that marvellous creature – Woman!

It was real, the laugh I heard, and the fragrance that came to me – real!

This fragrance was not of soap. Nor of oils. Nor was it the smell of powder mingling with sweat. But the amazing fragrance of Woman Incarnate!

I tried to evoke that fragrance ... I could hardly breathe. My nostrils expanded again and yet again. As if they would burst with desire. Where are you, woman?

I asked, "Where did it come from, that woman's laugh?"

The warder asked mockingly, "Not married, are you?"

"No, but what does that have to do with my question?"

"Why else would you pay attention to things like that?"

"In this terrifying Central Jail, close to the gallows, I hear a woman's laugh. Now should I get married immediately, just to have the right to ask where it came from?"

The warder laughed. "From the women's jail. You are going to be kept next to it."

Just one wall in between!

And my sentence – two years of rigorous imprisonment and a fine of one thousand rupees. And if the fine was not paid, lift loads for six more months. And between me and the women's jail, just a wall, right?

A wall ... the women's jail. Oh, my precious ones!

I hugged the blanket and rug to my heart as we walked on. Opening an iron-barred door, we entered a walled complex. Lots of trees, mostly jackfruit. Several cottages. In the distant east, on either sides, were two massive walls. Beyond the right wall was the wide, wide world of freedom. Across the wall on the left ... was the women's jail.

The cottages, encircled by small walls, were the lockups. There, the lockup warder took over. I folded my hands in a namaste to the warder who had accompanied me. He returned my greeting and left. A good man. May God protect him!

The new warder took me to a cottage. He opened its iron door. A very small room. Outside the room, at a distance, was the toilet. Near the door was a tap. I turned the tap and washed my hands and feet and face. After drinking a lot of water and filling a bowl with some more, I uttered the name of God and entered the mini-jail with my right foot.

Walls, walls! Many, many walls enclosed me.

The warder shut the iron-barred door and locked it.

I said, "This new dependent of our beloved sarkar has not been given any dinner."

"You did not fall into today's quota officially. You will be fed from tomorrow."

"Then let me go. I'll come back in tomorrow's quota."

He asked me, "What is the case?"

"Writing ... sedition."

As if frightened out of his wits, he exclaimed, "Sedition! Shri Padmanabha! Protect me!"

A true patriot!

Author's Note: I was brought to the Thiruvananthapuram Central Jail from the Kollam Kasba lockup. This was when Maharaja Sri Chitra Tirunal ruled over Travancore.

Translator's Note: Shri Padmanabha Swami (Vishnu) is the presiding deity of the Travancore royal family. The author's note contextualizes the warder's exclamation, identifying him as a native of Travancore.

Outside and above the iron bars of the lockup, an unbearably bright bulb came on. I was alone in this little prison within the vast prison of the universe. Eternity and myself.

I straightened the rug. Arranged the vessels in a corner. Dusk was falling. The interior of the lockup, including me, was brightly lit. And I did not even fall in today's quota! That meant going to sleep hungry. I knew very well how to get some food. I could shake the iron bars, yell for the warder and create a terrible racket. The superintendent, the jailor and everyone else would turn up. And I would be fed.

But I decided against it. One must make some small sacrifice for the sake of Literature. In the cause of the country's freedom, I have been beaten up several times. With great tenderness, I have been pushed to the ground by rifle butts in my chest and dragged through the streets. And several times I have landed in jail. But this time? This time, a prison sentence for Literature itself! ... And politics too. When I thought about it, I felt some pride.

I drank a lot of water. Then, in royal style, forgetting to split the match stick into two, I used a whole stick to light a beedi. After a few puffs, I stubbed it out and put it away. I must not be greedy.

Sitting there, I listened. I could no longer hear the woman's laugh. Could not sense that woman's smell. And here I was, near the women's jail. Woman, where are you?

That primeval smell of woman – could I have imagined it? Long, long ago ... aeons ago, before the age of Manu ... walking in the Garden of Eden as Adam, I had experienced that mysterious fragrance of Hauwa! The scent may have remained, stored in my soul ... a mere mirage, like the pool of clear water an exhausted wanderer sees in the desert ... And like a mirage it had vanished ... But my awakened soul, widening nostrils, my heart which was about to break ... Oh woman!

Where was that lovely sound? And where, where was that maddening fragrance?

I looked out through the iron bars. The light was so dazzling that I could not see at all. The world was covered with darkness. But it was a darkness I could not clearly see. One thing I came to understand then – I had never seen darkness. O primeval, deep, amazing darkness! O millions of stars that twinkle and flash in the endless vastness of the skies! O glorious, glorious, moon-drenched night! Why have I never seen you?

But that was not correct. I had seen it. I had seen it all. But I had never paid enough attention. Yamini! Night herself! I remembered another lovely night long ago. A little village. Beyond it, thousands of miles of desert filled with sand, stretching to the farthest horizon. A dusk like this one. I had gone into that desert. I must have walked a mile or so. White silk lay spread all around ... an endless expanse of sand. And I, in the centre of that vast universe ... Alone. Above my head, so close that I could have plucked it, hung the full moon, radiant. The deep blue sky, as if swept and scoured clean. The full moon and the stars. Stars sharply defined in their brightness. Crores ... endless crores ... impossible to count. The perfect circle of the moon. The perfect silence of the universe ... and yet, some kind of celestial, silent music ... the music of the spheres in their eternal orbits ... everything was steeped in it.

I stood in joyous amazement. My happiness and surprise turned to tears. I cried. Unable to bear it any more, I ran back, sobbing, to the world of humans.

Creator of the worlds, protect me. It is impossible for me to contain this within myself. This blinding brightness of yours, this grand miracle. I am but a small creature. I cannot bear it. Save me!

The next thing I remember is the jail warder unlocking the door in the morning and shaking the bars to wake me.

Salaam, world! I got up. Lighting a beedi, I started my morning ablutions in style. I cleaned my teeth with a neem twig. Long ago, in the valleys of the Himalayas, I had used neem twigs like this. Standing under the pipe, I bathed luxuriously. Then I put on my jail clothes, picked up the bowl for food after washing it, and set off to meet the leaders. Everybody there was a leader.

After I had met the leaders, a large bowl of kanji arrived. I ate my portion with substantial helpings of chutney. Actually, it was more like "kanjo." Let me tell you what this kanjo is. First swallow the watery portion of the kanji. Then mix the remaining rice with chutney and feed on that to your heart's content. After that you must wash your hands, mouth, and the bowl. Drink some water ... What bliss!

After working up this euphoria, I slit a match stick into two, lit a beedi, and took a drag. Then stubbing it, I went out to explore the world. That is, I made a tour of the jail. In search of tea leaves and sugar. Even though I was in jail, I needed my tea. Black tea would do.

The leaders had neither tea leaves nor sugar. One of these great souls had hidden away a bottle of Eno's Fruit Salt in his cell. Without it, he could not even begin his usual routine in the morning. Another had managed to secrete Karl Marx's magnum opus, *Das Kapital*. Another interesting leader possessed two packs of cards, and even promised to teach me the amazing game of bridge.

I avoided the leaders.

After a month, there was I, leading a "deluxe life."

In a corner of my cage were two bricks. Next to them was a bundle of twigs almost as thick as the trunk of a jackfruit tree. Also, a small vessel to make tea in. Tea and sugar in two paper packets reposed in all their glory under my mattress, like two tiny pillows. Then a deluxe chakki. Plenty of beedis. Paper to write on. Pencils. A big knife, a special concession from the jail superintendent ... for grafting mango trees. He had realized that I was adept at gardening. In front of the lockup, my mini-jail, I have made a rectangular patch fringed by rose plants in full bloom, spreading their fragrance.

Fried fish for lunch, eggs, liver, a special chutney ... A day in this life of lordly prosperity begins with a worthy soul bringing in my kanji in the morning. He happens to be a red-cap. That is, he has killed someone. He wasn't hanged, but was awarded rigorous imprisonment for life. He is a stout, fair, round-faced man with smiling eyes.

I perform a few exercises in the morning. After all, I am a wrestler of some repute. Next to my rose garden is a tall jackfruit tree. Its lower branch is as thick as my thigh. I use that as an exercise bar. By the time I emerge from my exercises and a bath, the red-cap with smiling eyes has left my daily quota of kanji and special chutney in a covered dish in the lockup. This repast is not exactly in the kanji department. But more like rice. Then again, is it really rice? The stuff is a little watery.

The first time the red-cap poured out the kanji for me, he suggested softly, "Go and see the hospital orderly. He will arrange for tea!"

I went. I saw. A thin, dark man with a stylish moustache. Dazzling white teeth. A beautiful smile. He turned out to be an old friend of mine. I had once visited his hometown. He was implicated in a case of arson. Two people had been killed. Again, a red-cap. Sentenced to rigorous imprisonment for life. He had been made a hospital orderly for good behaviour, also because he was educated. No further need to worry about procuring tea-leaves, sugar, eggs, liver, bread, milk, beedis and other such etceteras.

As I walked back, I saw a rose plants blooming riotously behind the hospital. I had pulled out some plants from there and gently transplanted them in the patch in front of my little jail. Seeing my garden, all the leaders wanted one each. I made gardens for all of them.

The leaders kept in touch with the world outside. The jail warders would carry letters in and out for a price. At night, various packets would be thrown in from over the high walls. The leaders would collect them in the morning. Banana chips – the salty kind as well as sharkara upperi, the jaggery-coated ones – lemon pickle, and other eatables. Sometimes I would join them in picking up small tins and containers. One day, a leader gave me some lemon pickle. Oh how tasty it was!

The look on his face as he gave it to me ... even if I were to write an epic poem on that expression, I would not be able to repay my debt.

And so there I was, with my comrades and disciples, the red-caps. A life free of stress and strain.

Sometimes I would look towards the women's jail. Those frightening, fiendish walls! I would remember the laugh I had heard. And the smell. At other times, I would climb the jackfruit tree. This was usually in the afternoon when, after lunch, the leaders and others would doze for a while. I would stand on the topmost branch of the tree and gaze at the free world far beyond.

"The free world!" But what free world? The entire globe is a prison after all. Over the brick walls ... far away in the distance ... on the road ... men and women walk, completely unaware of the existence of this jail. Comrades, turn your heads just a little. I address the women. Please, turn your heads a little. Let me refresh my eyes with a glimpse of womankind!

These were the sentiments of each man in the jail. Every thought and feeling I express would be echoed by each one of the inmates. Our lonely nights, our lonely thoughts, our sexual fantasies ... It would be better not to delve too deep into our hearts.

After long musings, I would climb down and just stand in the middle of my rose garden. All around me, flowers spread their fragrance. There was beauty. There was fragrance. Yet I felt the lack of someone or something. What could it be? No, stop it! These thoughts were dangerous. They all led to Woman.

I went for a walk. There were several walls. Several doors. Warders everywhere. It was impossible to do anything in jail without their knowledge. There were large towers too, to keep an eye from above.

I was walking around the towers. Suddenly I saw something. And burst out laughing. Such a funny sight! A mad elephant in fetters. No, it was a man. A black-cap. Fair, tall, well-built. Radiant eyes. As he approached, he staggered, his head pulled back and his body arched backwards. His strange gait was because of the two chains that went over his back to fetter his feet to his neck. I wondered if he was a convict who had attempted a jail break.

When I reached him, I was shocked to find that he was an old classmate of mine. Our eyes met. Our minds remembered. We laughed. Spoke of many things. Laughed again. Our man had set forth to somehow meet me. Secretly!

I asked him, "Couldn't you have just sent someone?"

"Wouldn't it have been embarrassing for you if people found out that I know you?"

"Know me? Say that I am your friend, you old rascal, you idiot!"

I hugged him and gave him a kiss on the cheek. I might as well have kissed every single person in jail. The story of the kiss spread, the entire jail was thrilled by it!

The chap, a thief, had been sentenced to one-and-a-half years of imprisonment. He had started a flourishing business in beedis, sugar and dried fish in the jail. Soon, he of the radiant eyes, now in chains, had become a living legend in this jail. A martyr because of a small incident that took place six months after he came to the jail. One of the warders did something terrible. No other warder had ever done such a thing before. Let us call him the "Terrible Warder."

Almost all the warders have a share in the business conducted in jail. Many prisoners are taken out, far from the jail, to break rocks and do similar jobs. In those places, there are many inhabited huts. That is where the major business takes place. And so, my classmate became one of the big businessmen in jail. Most things come into jail via the langoti. An inspection is carried out at the gate. The cap, shirt, mundu, towel are provided by the jail. All these are checked thoroughly. Nothing there. Clean! But the langoti, the underwear which is almost a part of the human body, is not given by the authorities. So it is slipped off just a little. A quarter of a minute will do. And so the tale proceeds.

All this is immaterial, really. Didn't I say that our Terrible Warder did something terrible, almost unspeakable? Well, my classmate planted two hefty blows on his pate for it! The news spread. Not just in the men's jail, but also in the women's jail. There was much excitement in both places. My classmate was tied to the flogging frame and given twelve lashes. His sentence was increased to three years. His wounds healed. He wanted to go back to breaking rocks. But the Terrible Warder was against it.

"You don't know me. And you don't know where I come from. Here, take this!" With this spirited introduction, my classmate again administered the Terrible Warder two solid ones on his throat. And as a finishing touch, a hefty kick on the navel. There was nothing wrong with such behaviour. Outside the jail, the Terrible Warder would have been lynched for his deed! That should tell you how hideous his act was.

My classmate got another twenty-four lashes. He bore it all stoically. Didn't faint. His sentence was extended to six years. The Terrible Warder was boycotted by the entire jail. He became the target of the prisoners' collective wrath. He could see the lust for blood gleam in each eye. What if he were strangled to death? Realizing the gravity of the situation, he claimed to have urgent business outside and resigned his job.

You know the common saying, "Unity is strength." Well, in jail, we did stand united! Even though he was no longer allowed to go out to break stones, my classmate continued to run the business in jail.

So I live, in supreme happiness. I have everything I need.

Sometimes the assistant jailer comes to my lockup. He is a fair young man with a sense of humour, dressed in khaki trousers and khaki shirt. He sports a hat! All the prisoners call him Anian Jailor. He

---

Anian: Younger brother.

comes not to inspect my lockup, but to chat. He has a young Alsatian dog called Joker. We discuss Joker's training, exercise and food habits. Anian loves to hear my dog stories. I make him black tea.

Most people know that I have tea leaves and sugar. Sometimes men who are to be hanged at five in the morning feel like a little tea the night before. The warder wakes me up and I send them some black tea. Along with a couple of beedis and matches. I also send a message that they should be brave. There are two ways of facing death, laughing or crying ... either way one dies. In that case, why not face death laughing!

On such occasions I stay awake. Only after the hanging at five do I go to sleep. Just as I am about to drop off, one of the leaders comes and wakes me up. Not out of spite. After all, the others don't know that I have been keeping a death vigil!

Altogether, the jail is like a small town. Debates and discussions Bursts of laughter. Arguments. Noise, bustle, more laughter.

Sometimes the jail superintendent accompanies Anian Jailor. After talking to the leaders, they come to my garden. I am very fond of trees and plants. To the extent that I believe they understand me when I speak to them. The jail superintendent shares my sentiments. We stroll around, chatting about what fertilizers to use, how to tend to the plants.

The superintendent has six potted rose plants at home. All of them have been sent by yours truly. Some of my red-cap friends do not approve of my friendship with the jail superintendent. They ask me all sorts of questions. Can't you live here without his patronage? Wasn't it he who sentenced your classmate to be lashed two dozen times? That Anian Jailor is a much nicer fellow!

Do you see where all this is leading to? You have to affiliate yourself to one party or the other. It is impossible to stay detached and independent and love everyone.

Most of the time I was in my cage. At times I strolled in my garden, talking to plants and trees. One day, at such a time, Anian Jailor came and told me that all political prisoners were to be freed!

Everybody was jubilant. Everybody had a haircut and a shave. Including yours truly who got the sparse hair on his bald pate trimmed. But I didn't have my moustache shaved. I was happy in the belief that I looked good with it. There was laughter and bustle all around. Anian Jailor had everyone's clothes brought to them. We got them washed and ironed, and kept them ready wrapped in paper.

I bid farewell to my friends who were thieves and murderers. I said that I would write to all of them and promised to send them books. We waited impatiently for our release.

The release order arrived.

Release! Except for one person! There was no order for the release of this poor chap. It must be a mistake! Anian Jailor rushed to find out. He got the superintendent to make a special phone call for me.

There was no mistake. This man was not to be released. Good. That meant I had not yet attained the level of maturity they wanted.

The leaders left, rejoicing. And there I was, the sole heir to Eno's Fruit Salt, Karl Marx's tome, two packs of cards, a small bottle of lemon pickle, a sweet-tin full of banana chips, a large palm-leaf bundle of sharkara upperi, lots of pounded tobacco, betel leaves, supari, lime.

The leaders all left with smiles ... Nothing stirred anywhere. It was as if I was alone in a deserted town. In any case one is alone in this wide world. From the entire flock sent out to graze, just one old goat had been kept back. For what? To be butchered, certainly. A disaster loomed ahead, I felt. No happiness, no smiles, no nothing. Altogether, there was a sort of twilight in my heart.

I gave Karl Marx's *Das Kapital* to Anian Jailor. And the sharkara upperi to the hospital to be distributed among my fellow inmates. I gave the packs of cards as a special gift to my classmate. The betel leaves and all that went with it were donated to my disciple, the red-cap who brings my kanji. By and by, I distributed most of the banana chips. Only half a tin was left. The lemon pickle and Eno's Fruit Salt remained in my room. After a couple of days, I threw the Eno's Fruit Salt over the wall of the jail. And I lived on, in fear and foreboding.

I had no peace of mind. What was to happen to me? It is easy to advise others. Face death bravely, and so on. About laughing and crying. Now face it laughing! God, I cannot even smile. I am such a completely insignificant person, utterly helpless. Save me. What am I to do?

Escape! I decided to break out of jail. There were just two walls between me and the world outside. I must tunnel my way through one and climb over the other. The jail warder would be asleep at night. Let night come, a night of rain and wind and lightning, a deep dark night.

I planned the minutest details. The walls of my small lockup are not very thick. I have an instrument with which to bore through them. In the quiet of the night, I will get out. And there will only be the high old stone wall of the jail. Between the ancient stones, there is just gravel.

I need some ten or twelve large nails. These have to be hammered into the wall with a stone wrapped in cloth to avoid making any noise. I will climb them to reach the top of the wall. With the rug, blanket, mundu, towel, I will make a rope, tie one end of it to a nail, then lower the rope carefully over the other side, climb down and escape. The plan should work.

But the nails? In a corner, next to the wall, lie several rusty iron buckets. They are falling apart, but the handles are undamaged. I hammered them straight, shaping them into the nails I wanted, and carefully hid them away. About thirty nails. Then I waited. I waited for a night of rain and lightning and howling wind.

And so arrived another dawn. A number of the red-caps who are my friends and disciples arrived with a warder. They were going to make a vegetable garden near the women's jail. Would I like to come?

No. I'm not interested in anything. All the warmth and light has gone from my life. Just go away, all of you. Who wants your vegetables? All I'm waiting for is a night of wind and rain and the rumbling of thunder. Stop bothering me!

But they wouldn't let me alone. Why should you withdraw from society like some sage?

Well, that's what I am, a muni who meditated with his guru in a dark cave long ago!

I went along. We made a garden. And then a friend showed me something interesting. At the bottom of the reddish wall was a large black, pappadam-like circle, blocked with cement. Earlier it had been a large hole. Born of many moments, many hours, many days, many months of love-inspired hard labour by many men. And there it had stayed. For days, months, years.

Meanwhile, the prisoners became decent and obedient. Through that hole the men's jail and the women's jail had seen faces and things ... faces and things. Had heard sounds. Had taken in the scent. Good! Through that hole, the smell of woman had spread in the men's jail. Marvellous! Not that this had been some well-kept secret. The business had been conducted under the benign, neglectful eyes of the authorities.

At this point you might want to set yourself on some high pedestal and deliver a fantastic lecture on morality and culture. Oh, go away! You of the great soul and perfect qualities, we are mere human beings, full of lust and anger. We have many a weakness. Show us some pity. This attraction between man and woman is a gift of God, right? Attraction! Don't forget that. You must look upon us with the gaze of divine understanding.

They used the hole. Looked through it. Everyone looked. But the Terrible Warder had seen a nice little business there. He levied a small tax on looking through the hole. One anna per person. The prison had both rich and poor inmates. Their sexual desires are the same. What were the poor to do? Was it to be the death of their lust!

My classmate said, "Warder, this isn't fair."

"If it isn't fair, I'll just plug the hole!" threatened the Terrible Warder. This was how my classmate received four-and-a-half years and thirty-six lashes. And then he got the hole closed with cement. That cement wasn't mixed with the blood of men and women! Yet , I bent my head and sniffed at the cemented portion. Was there a hint of a female fragrance still?

We reared our vegetable garden with great zest. The area around my lockup was deserted. Just me and a sleepy warder. I was alone inside a large, walled structure!

Two or three fellows would come in the morning to water the vegetable garden. I would just stroll around with a warder in tow. It was as if I was walking the streets of a ruined, deserted city. Gloom, silence everywhere. I would suddenly stop while walking. Was the silence going to deepen? I would whistle. Speak to the trees and plants. There were a lot of squirrels. I caught one. Decided to tame it. Made it run up a tree. Then tried to make it fall.

One day, as I walked along the wall of the women's prison, whistling to myself, I heard a heavenly melody. It was the most beautiful sound in all the world. It came from the other side of the wall ... And then, came a question, "Who's whistling like that?"

It was like a sudden burst of light and fragrance. A miracle! My hair stood on end. I looked around. Then summoning up courage, I said, "It is me!"

I shivered. Ah Woman!

The conversation had to be quite loud. She, on one side of the wall. I, on the other.

She asked me, "What's your name?"

I told her about my education, my job, my seditious writings, everything. She too told me about herself, the mistakes she had made in her life.

Her lovely name, Narayani.

Her lovely age, twenty-two.

She knew how to read and write. She had had a little education. Sentenced to fourteen years of rigorous imprisonment, it had been a year since she arrived here. One year of no happiness!

I said, "Narayani, we seem to have come to this jail at about the same time."

"Is that so?" There was silence for a while from the other side. Then she asked, "Will you give me a rose plant?"

I was surprised. "How did you know about the rose plants here?"

"This is a jail! Everyone knows everything. There are no secrets here."

Did you hear what she said? No secrets here! But what do I know about the women's jail? About the women there?

Narayani asked again, "Won't you give me a rose plant?"

"Narayani!" I said with all my strength, as if my heart was being plucked out. "I will give you all the rose plants in this entire world!"

Narayani laughed. The sound was like the tinkling of a thousand little golden bells. As I heard the sound, my heart felt as if it had been shattered into millions of tiny pieces.

"One will do. Just one. Will you give it to me?"

Listen to her! She asks me if I will give her one rose plant! What am I to do with this Narayani? Hold her tightly and kiss her so hard that she becomes breathless, what else!

"Narayani!" I called out, "Wait. I'll go and get one right away!"

"All right."

I rushed to my garden. Seeing me, all the squirrels ran away and climbed up the trees! I scolded them, "What's the matter with you, you stupid creatures! Clambering up trees like this? Just get down and walk around, you hear!"

I reached my rose garden. All the bushes were in bloom, smiling, bathed in sunlight ... I uprooted the most beautiful one, with the maximum number of branches, taking care to protect its roots with a large yam-like covering of mud. Covered this up with a piece of sacking. Smoothed all the twigs and tied them together. Then I ran to the wall.

"Narayani!"

No answer. Had she left?

"Narayani!" I called again.

The sound of laughter.

Then, a voice. "What?"

"Where were you when I first called?"

"I was right here!"

"Well, why didn't you answer then?"

"I was hiding!"

"You little rogue!"

She laughed and asked, "Have you brought the rose plant?"

I was silent. Soundlessly, I was planting kisses. On each rose, on each bud, on each shoot.

Narayani called out to me by name.

I didn't answer. I was busy planting kisses. On each thorn, each branch. Again Narayani called out my name with anxiety. This time I answered.

Perplexed at that, she said, "If I had called upon God with such love..."

"And if you had?"

She snapped, "If I had called out to God with such love ... that is what I said!"

"And if you had called out to God with such love?"

"God would have become visible to me!"

"Is that so?... But Narayani, God does not become visible to anybody! God is with us always. In the universe, in the light of the universe, its radiance ... Narayani! Isn't it I who have to become visible?"

"Then why didn't you answer?"

"I was kissing ..."

"The wall?"

"No."

"Then?"

"Each rose and each branch and each leaf."

Narayani said, "Oh! I feel like crying."

I called, "Narayani!"

"What!"

"You must not remove the sacking. Dig a hole and place it inside, taking the name of God. Then fill the hole and water it."

"Hmm."

"Okay here it comes!" Holding the bundle by the top, I threw it over the wall with all my strength. "Have you got it?"

"Oh my God!" exclaimed Narayani, and in her voice was the happiness of having gained an empire.

I said, "Untie the branches."

"I'll do that. I'm going to pluck out all the flowers and put them away."

"Where? In you hair?"

"No."

"Then."

"In my heart. Inside my blouse."

And they had my kisses! I leaned weakly against the wall. I stroked it gently.

Narayani said, "I'll go and plant this and water it. You must always look towards the wall. Whenever I am here, you will find a dry twig above the wall. When you see it will you come?"

"I will!"

It sounded like she was sobbing.

"Ohh ... my god!"

"What is it, Narayani?"

She replied, "I feel like crying!"

I asked, "But why?"

Narayani said, "I don't know!"

I said, "Go, plant it and come back."

"I'll throw up a dry twig!"
"And I'll look out for it."
"When you see it, will you come?"
"I will!"

I went back to my lockup. What a mess it was in! I cleaned it. It had been ages since I had shaken out my mattress and made my bed. Then, with my gaze fixed on the sky above the wall in the distance, I began to wait. I saw no twig. Had she forgotten about me? That dry twig would never rise against the sky ... Just as I had begun to despair – Oh celestial world! A beautiful sight! A twig rose against the sky! I didn't stir. Again it flashed. I dashed as fast as I could to the wall. Several squirrels fled for their lives up trees, and cursed me roundly.

"Narayani!"

Silence on the other side of the wall! I called again. Finally, she answered angrily, "What is it? What do you want?"

"Oh!"

"My arm has almost fallen off from flinging twigs!"

"Come, I'll stroke and make it better."

"Here's my arm. Stroke it! I've put it close against the wall."

"I'm stroking it now. And kissing it."

"I'm pressing my breast against the wall ... and kissing you!" she said.

"Narayani, how many women are there in the jail?"

She laughed. "Just me!"

"Little liar! Seriously, how many?"

"Lots. All of them are old hags!"

"How many?"

"Eighty-seven."

"How many beauties, how many hags?"

"One beauty and eighty-six hags!"

I gave up. I asked, "Aren't there rose plants in your jail?"

"No," said Narayani. "You know, I ... are you listening?"

"Yes."

"Tomorrow I'll toss you a bag of roasted and powdered bajra. You must eat it with jaggery. Will you?"

"Of course!"

"No!" she said with certainty, "You'll throw it away!"

"I won't waste even a grain!"

"What is your face like?"

"It is longish. Fair. My hair is cropped. I'm a little bald."

"Eyes?"

"Rather small, elephant eyes."

"Mine are large elephant eyes. Chest?"

"Somewhat broad."

"My chest is full too. Waist?"

"My waist is trim."

"And my waist? Well, I don't feel like telling you!"

"Must be like a barrel!"

"I could scratch you and tear you to pieces!" she growled.

"Narayani!"

"What?"

"What colour are you?"

"Where?"

"On your beautiful face."

"Sort of fair."

"Narayani!"

"Yes?"

"I could get the smell of a woman!"

"Right now? Oh my god!"

"No, when I came into this jail and was walking here!"

"Could it have been mine?"

"I don't know."

"The smell of male bodies ... the smell there, what is it like?"

"I don't know. Narayani! The smell of your body!"

I widened my nostrils and inhaled deeply. Had she heard the intake of my breath?

She asked, "Can you get the smell?"

"No."

"Nor can I. This damned wall!"

"Narayani, there used to be a hole in this wall. Have you seen it?"

"I have seen the part that has been blocked with cement. I have even touched it. It was closed before I came here."

"I tried smelling there!"

"The warder who closed it was beaten up by someone. I heard that the man who beat him was tied to the frame and lashed. Each stroke was painfully counted by the women here!"

"He was tied to the frame and given thirty-six lashes! Here too, the men counted each one with pain."

"It's a shame."

"The man who was thrashed is from my hometown. He was my classmate."

"Really?"

"Really."

And over the wall appeared a long, rounded, white cloth-bag. In it was roasted and powdered bajra. Chillies, fried and salted, also arrived. Lemon pickle went over to the other side. And the tin of banana chips.

Narayani asked, "Can I ... distribute ... these chips?"

"Yes, do give them to everyone. From both of us."

"Will you love me ... and me only?"

"Why, do you doubt it?"

"Here," said Narayani with some pain, "There are many who are more beautiful than me. I'm not very beautiful."

"Nor am I very handsome."

She said, "I want to see you."

I said, "And I want to see you."

"Oh my god! I'll cry all night."

The night of wind and rain and thunder is here! I'm sitting in the iron-barred cage, bathed in light. The rain falls like rods of glass. Like showers of gravel. The blessing of God. Let it rain! Blow, stormy wind. But please don't pluck out any trees! Clouds, thunder softly, softly. This rude roaring of yours might frighten the poor women! So, softly ...

With morning, the warder arrived, switched off the lights and unlocked my door. I stepped outside. The world was washed clean.

I felt suddenly that it was not such a good idea to escape from jail! What was I going to do outside? After all, what is called the free world is only a larger jail. There would be more nights of rain and thunder and wind and lightning. I put out of my mind the memory of where I had hidden the big nails. In short, I was convinced it was adharma to contemplate escaping from prison!

The wall may not be flesh and blood. But I was beginning to wonder if it did not have a soul. These walls had seen much. Heard much.

One day, I saw a large squirrel sitting on top of the wall. He was glaring at me! I said, "Get down, you scoundrel. Have you no shame?"

Narayani asked, "Whom are you scolding?"

"A squirrel. He's sitting on the wall and listening to us. The rogue!"

"Let him be," said Narayani.

"He has come to laugh at me. I have often given him and his friends the chase of their lives!"

I threw gravel at him. The squirrel ran away.

Narayani complained, as if in pain, "That stone hit my breast!"

"Did it hurt?"

"Is there no way we can get to see each other?"

"I don't really see any way!"

"I'll cry tonight, thinking of you!"

I too thought of her that night and dreamed my dreams.

So the nights and days passed.

"I'll try to come to the hospital!" said Narayani one day. "If you can ... will you come to the hospital to see me? I want to see you, even if from a distance!"

"I'll come running up to you and hold you tight and kiss you. On your face, and your neck, and your breasts, your navel ..."

"How will you recognize me?"

"I'll know you by your face!"

Narayani said, "On my right cheek I have a black mole. Will you look out for it?"

"That black mole! I want to shower kisses on it!"

"You must come. Don't let me down. There will be other women with me."

"I will be alone. I won't be wearing my cap. I am a little bald. And I'll be carrying a red rose in my hand."

"I'll look out for that!"

"The orderly at the hospital is an old friend of mine."

"I guessed as much."

"Why?"

"How else would you get eggs, liver, bread. If I die will you think of me?"

"Do you want any more rose plants? There are many here."

"No. From what you gave me, I have started making a garden ... Will you remember me when I am dead?"

"My dear Narayani! It isn't possible to say anything about death. Who will die, when, how – only God knows these things. It could be me who dies first."

"No. It will be me. Will you remember me?"

"I will."

"How? Oh god! How will you remember me? You haven't seen me, touched me."

"Narayani, your image is everywhere in this world!"

She asked sorrowfully, "Everywhere in this world? Why do you flatter me?"

"I'm not flattering you. I swear! Walls, walls!"

I stood looking at the walls. A long silence came from the other side.
Then Narayani said, "Can I cry to my heart's content?"
"Not now. You can cry at night, remembering."
Silence. Then she said, "I'll tell you tomorrow when we can meet at the hospital."
We parted, with longing in our hearts.

A still from the Malayalam film, *Mathilukal.* Directed by Adoor Gopalakrishnan
and featuring Mammootty, the film won a National Award in 1989
and the UNICEF and Sipresci awards in 1990.

Night fell. The light came on. The warder came. The light was switched off. The door opened. I stepped out. Quickly finished brushing my teeth, exercising, bathing. Managed to eat a bit. Lit a beedi. And so I waited, smoking. Anian Jailor arrived to ask after me. It was then that a dry twig rose against the blue sky over the wall.

I broke into a sweat. I could hardly breathe. What was I to do?

At last! Anian Jailor left. I ran.

"Narayani!"

"What?"

"When?"

Narayani said, "Today's Monday. On Thursday morning, at eleven. I will be at the hospital. A black mole on the right cheek. Don't forget!"

"I'll remember. And in my hand, a red rose."

"I'll remember!"

Monday, Tuesday, Wednesday ... I dozed off a little after lunch. Awoke and took a bath. And as I was sitting around, Anian Jailor walked smiling into my rose garden, plucked several blooms, and coming into my lockup, sat on my bed. "Do you want some flowers?" he asked.

I was amused. I said, "I am the garden. And the flower."

"Not the fruit?"

"The fruit too!"

And suddenly I spotted the dry twig flash above the wall, against the blue sky!

Anian Jailor said, "I haven't ever seen you in ordinary dress."

"You mean a kurta and mundu."

Anian Jailor took out the packet in which my laundered clothes were kept.

"Please put them on. I want to see how you look."

"But they will get soiled."

"So what? Can't you get them washed?"

"All right." I put on my clothes. "What do you say?" I asked.

"Fine!" said Anian Jailor happily.

Then in a dramatic manner, in English, he announced, "You can go, Mr Basheer. You are free!"

I was stunned. My eyes stopped seeing. My ears stopped hearing. I was dazed. "Why should I be free ... who wants freedom?"

Anian Jailor laughed. "The order for your release has arrived. You are free from this moment. You can go out into the free world."

"The free world ... which free world? I'd just be going into a bigger jail. Who wants this great freedom?"

Anian Jailor said, "You can collect the money to go home and leave. Do you have anything else to take?"

He folded up the mattress. Under it was the story I was writing for the lifers, called "Love Letter." He put it inside my pocket. Many other stories of mine were with the lifers still. It did not matter! Anian Jailor happily took my by the hand and led me out of the lockup.

I stood for a little while in my rose garden. As if in a dream, I broke off a flower and, kissing it, looked around. Above the wall was a dry twig! It rose. And rose ... Oh god!

Anian Jailor locked my room.

Well, Narayani, God be with you!

I stepped out of the large gates of the jail with the money to go home in my pocket. The monstrous gates clanged shut behind me, making a hideous noise.

I was alone. Looking at the fragrant rose I held in my hand, I stood on the road for a long while, stunned.

God be with all of us!

This story was first published as "Mathilukal" in 1965.

Anal Huq

Legend has it that when the government, and the religious high priests who stood by it, murdered Manzoor Al Hallaj, chopped and burned his body, and cast the ashes into the Euphrates, then that enraged river, like an ocean in fury, reverberated with the words "Anal Huq." Though the story of the river's fiery echo is exaggerated and countless are such incidents recorded in world history in the name of religion, the account of Manzoor's life does arouse terror and fury.

The charge against Manzoor was that he was in the habit of uttering Anal Huq, Anal Huq. The words have the same sense as "Aham Brahmasmi" or "I am the truth." In effect, Manzoor was saying that he was God: This was like a drop of water in the ocean claiming to be the ocean, or a grain of sand in the mountain saying it was the mountain.

Had Manzoor really said such a thing? Even if he had, his claims could have been dismissed as the utterances of a madman.

But then Manzoor was not a madman. He was a Sufi advocate for the divine spirit of man. Perhaps what he meant was that as God's creation, man too has the divine spark in him. However, the consequences of this assertion were appallingly gruesome.

translated by
Vanajam Ravindran

It was a time after Hijra, at the beginning of the fourth century, a time hostile to the evolution of ideas. The Persian kingdom, steeped in heady wine, the scent of roses, and embraces of beautiful courtesans, had fallen into dissolution. Learned people, religious leaders, poets and artists, cowered before a despotic ruler and were reduced to being mere sycophants. At such a time was Manzoor Al Hallaj born.

Manzoor grew up in the tranquil atmosphere of Baiza, a little village far from the vanity and pomp of the palace. When the contemplative, enquiring lad reached the threshold of youth, he managed to enter the reputed centre of learning in Tushtar, a neighbouring city. Though he acquired incomparable proficiency in Metaphysics, Religion, Politics and Literature, Manzoor left the portals of learning a dissatisfied and disillusioned scholar. He felt that he had learned nothing worthwhile and grew restless.

Possessed of a boundless urge to explore the Self, a burning desire to know and grasp it, he set out in search of self-knowledge. Ignorant, he groped in darkness. Despairing of being able to find a single ray of light, he wandered about as a fakir.

Then he met Umar Ibini Usman whose sanctuary seemed to him like an oasis in a desert. The preceptor pointed a new way to him – Sufism, the resplendent flood of spiritual knowledge. With the speed of a tempest, of fleeting Time, Manzoor plunged headlong into the new fount of knowledge. Transcending temporal and physical boundaries, he merged with the great bottomless light, like a speck of cloud.

One day, deep in meditation, Manzoor Al Hallaj was suddenly overcome by emotion. He cried out for the first time, Anal Huq, Anal Huq – I am the Eternal Reality, I am the Creator and the Creation.

The sanctuary experienced a tremor. Terror-stricken, the preceptor and his disciples stared at Manzoor. What an utterance! This one proclamation had shattered the very edifice of centuries-old human beliefs, of ancient human wisdom. "Anal Huq!" However, they sought consolation in the thought that Manzoor was eccentric. The preceptor advised him, "Manzoor, it is not right to regard the creator and the created as one and the same. It is a violation of the social law. Don't you realize that death is the penalty for a transgression of the Shariat?"

Death! A chill ran down his spine. Manzoor had not given a thought to the law of the land. But too soon, Manzoor forgot this threat and continued his spiritual quest with unabated fervour. Fearing that the sanctuary would be destroyed, the preceptor asked him to leave.

Out in the open, Manzoor was hounded and chased by a mob. They hurled stones at him as if he suffered from a contagious disease. Shunned by everybody, knowing it was impossible to remain in Basra, Manzoor wandered helplessly. He sought refuge in many hermitages, but in vain. At last he reached Baghdad, where he met Hazrat Junayid, the eminent Sufi scholar. The Hazrat welcomed Manzoor with a smile and granted him space in his sanctuary. But he also gently admonished Manzoor to keep his views to himself. Manzoor was stunned. "Is there not a patch of ground on this wide earth where man can breathe the refreshing air of freedom!" he wondered.

Yet, Manzoor soon established himself there. He was constantly engaged in metaphysical debates with Hazrat Junayid's disciples, feeling inspired in their midst. But the Hazrat warned him, his voice heavy with sorrow, "Manzoor, beware. The day is fast approaching when the white sands on the banks of the Euphrates will be tinged with red. Beware of that final day."

Manzoor was silent. "That final day ... I am not afraid of it, my master, " he said. "But you will have to step down from your state of eminence, discard the dervish's habit and become a mere executor of the law. You should be careful. Anal Huq."

The moving pages of history witnessed many more events. Manzoor came out of hiding. Temples, marketplaces, open grounds, all of them resounded with his eloquent preaching. People were attracted to this new interpretation of the divine. It caused a tempest in the world of ideas. One heard in it the war-cry of a revolution.

The religious leaders fell deep into thought about what was to happen in the future. They started plotting Manzoor's execution. He was called an infidel and an atheist. The rumours spread.

It was under these conditions that Manzoor travelled all over the country. He wrote many books – forty-seven in five years. Due to the government ban on them, these treatises gained wide publicity. Most intellectuals and poets, of course, did not fail to honour Manzoor. They called him an incomparable philosopher and poet.

The powerless government of the Sultan was alarmed at these developments, the opposition of the priestly order intensified. Now Manzoor had to reckon with two powerful enemies – authority and tradition. Then, in a strange volte face, the government tried to woo him to their side with promises of high state honours. Religious bodies made attempts to lure him into controversial debates.

Confronting a large gathering of religious scholars in Baghdad, Manzoor Al Hallaj said, "Human ideas cannot be contained within a fortress. Breaking all earthly barriers, they will fly in myriad directions. Since it is not possible for me to conform my ideals and views to your will and command, it is better that you do not consider me as one of your fold."

The wrathful eyes of a thousand priests turned towards Manzoor. Prompted by uncontrollable anger, one of them got up, pushed Manzoor to the floor and struck him. Gathering like vultures round the unconscious Manzoor, the priests unanimously drew up a fatwa against him. "Manzoor has violated the Shariat to become a kafir. As such he is liable to be put to death!"

Without registering a word of protest, more than a thousand ulemas became signatories to the fatwa. While Hameed Ibini Abbas, the minister of Baghdad, supported it, Sultan Muktabirbilla refused to do so. He insisted that he would not be a signatory to any fatwa that was not endorsed by Hazrat Junayid.

So, the representatives of the ulemas went to Hazrat Junayid's sanctuary six times to persuade him to sign the fatwa. But it was an exercise in futility. Eventually, the Caliph ordered Hazrat Junayid to state in unequivocal terms whether he was for or against the fatwa. Anguished, Hazrat Junayid cast off his ascetic's robe, donned the lawmaker's and signed the fatwa. Tears welling in his eyes, he wrote with a trembling hand, "In accordance with the social law, Manzoor is liable to receive a death penalty. But if it is on the basis of truth, only God can decide." Needless to say, in this world, social law wields authority over the law of God.

Manzoor was handcuffed and taken to the banks of the Euphrates by armed soldiers, tied to a cross, and subjected to all kinds of torture. But when he was finally incarcerated, he preached from behind the bars, attracting large crowds.

Public statements proclaiming Manzoor's innocence spread far and wide. The ulemas approached him. Hearing this news, the Sultan too arrived there. It was felt that prolonging Manzoor's confinement would only cause a law and order problem detrimental to public well-being. Therefore, the only solution was to put him to death without further delay.

The twenty-ninth day of the month of Dulkha-ad, Hijra 304, is a day that history remembers with a shudder. That day Manzoor Al Hallaj was brought out of captivity and the death sentence read out to him in the presence of thronging crowds.

Smiling, Manzoor said, "Anal Huq!"

A rain of blows fell on his back. He was stripped and made to stand in the blazing sun. As he was led to the gallows, the frenzied mob shouted at him. But to Manzoor, the gallows seemed like the very portals of heaven. Only the courageous are capable of such fortitude.

The executioners were waiting, ready to perform their task. While he was making his final supplication to God, stones came whizzing through the air and struck his body. The mob demanded that his limbs be chopped off.

As their behest was being carried out, Manzoor smiled and said softly that it was easy to destroy the physical body. To those who tried

to raise him, Manzoor said, "Let not my pale face see the world." They then gouged out his daring, unafraid eyes.

The mob roared, "Mince the kafir's tongue."

Manzoor Al Hallaj appealed to the people to pause a while so that he could make his final statement. Raising his sightless eyes towards the sky, he said, "O, ultimate object of my heart's desire, let not my tormentors be deprived of their happy fortune. Anal Huq."

An old woman came up to him, spat on his face and, pulling out his tongue, cut it off. And then his majestic head was severed from his body. The legend says that the irate mob was still not satisfied. It burned the hacked body and cast the ashes into the Euphrates.

And then, still, silent, nature witnessed the waters of the peaceful river suddenly turn bloody and violent. The waters swelled and surged like a furious ocean. Thundering, they roared, "Anal Huq."

"Anal Huq" was first published in the anthology *Anarghanimisham* (1946).

Authorial Note: I wrote this piece forty years ago. This is the year 1982. I believe it is presumptuous on the part of man, who is only one of God's creations, to say "Anal Huq" or "Aham Brahmasmi." The story of Manzoor is not drawn on historical facts. The whole thing may be treated as mere fantasy. Anal Huq.

The rightful inheritors of the earth

When I became the owner of a tiny little piece of this wide earth, I firmly believed that my future was secure. It was a two-acre plot with coconut palms and an old house that could be renovated ...

Those were the days when the price of coconuts was spiralling. I savoured the thought of the palms laden with coconuts. It was a happy existence ...

But then arrived the interlopers. Trespassing. Flouting the legality of the ownership documents. Violating the fence at the boundary. Defying the sentry, my dog Shan. They did not seem to care for anyone in the world, not even the government!

The first arrivals were birds and butterflies. A wide variety of birds. And so many, many butterflies! Perched on the boughs of the trees and plants, the birds chirped. The butterflies fluttered around in the courtyard, flashing their colours in the sunlight ...

The chirping birds and the butterflies could not be shooed off by us. But then came the crows ... Their raucous cawing was more insufferable than the racket of other birds. Besides, they swooped down on the chicks.

They were followed by the hawks that perched on the coconut palms with the same intent. They kept watch and waited ...

Soon there were mongooses in the bamboo thicket. And foxes in the shrubbery patch near it, ready to pounce on the hens ...

translated by
Vanajam Ravindran

Even as I wondered what right these creatures had to be on my land, there emerged a fierce creature without hands or legs or wings ... a cobra. It stood before me, dignified, majestic, its hood spread out as if asking me what business I had on this patch.

I said, "You had better leave my two-acre land. Immediately."

But then, where could it go ... Hadn't almost the whole of this earth been bought by man, bit by bit?

My wife said, "The jackfruit has ripened. But squirrels and crows are feasting on it. The guavas, sapotas and graft mangoes are all being eaten up by birds and bats."

"But that's the beauty of it," I remarked. "God almighty, who holds the universe together without a single prop, has created a variety of things for His creatures – fruit, edible roots, grass, grain, flowers, water, air, warmth and light. Don't you think we should remind ourselves always that birds, beasts and insects too are entitled to the produce of the earth?"

Almighty God, how unfortunate it is that rats have to be killed so that we can live. Can human beings not survive without destroying other creatures of the earth? ...

What we need is a scientific method, a novel idea which will make it possible for us to live without killing any creatures ...

O Creator of Rats, bear with us. They are going to be exterminated. Through treachery. The issue is the loss of nine hundred coconuts every month, the sole means of our livelihood. Forgive us, forgive us.

After shopping for two hours, my wife returned home. Along with other items of purchase was a large tin of rat poison ... The poison was mixed with bananas, rice, tapioca, and kept all over the place. Beneath the coconut palms as well.

In four days, five hens, twelve squirrels, two hundred rats and a cat disappeared behind the curtains of Time for ever. Dead rats rotted in the attic. Death was everywhere. The stench spread all over the house.

But the tender coconuts continued to fall. A fortnight passed. The coconut-palm climbers then said, "The owls are the culprits. They peck at the tender coconuts."

But that was really an old saying, a myth they had heard from their fathers ... The owl is not a vegetarian creature.

After a couple of months, the real culprits were discovered – the bats. After dusk, huge bats come in swarms and cling to the tender coconuts. They gnaw into the tender flesh and have their fill of coconut water. After eating the kernels, they fly away, gratified ...

"Let's buy a gun," said my wife. "We can shoot bats, foxes and polecats with it."

"Not me. I shall not be a party to that. The gun is a symbol of cruelty. It is the child of sin. Man should never have invented it."

My wife's cousin turned up one day with an expensive, grim-looking gun and said, "Within a ten-mile circumference, nearly three thousand coconuts are being destroyed every day. There is no point in shooting the bats at this spot. On a little islet nearby, stands an old temple. Next to it grow a pair of banyan trees. You can see at least three thousand bats hanging on the two trees. I'll finish them off. If not in one day, in two to three days. Don't you want to witness the glorious sight of three thousand bats being slaughtered?"

I prayed fervently, "Oh bats, save yourselves."

It was astonishing. A miracle! The bats were saved.

My wife and cousin returned shamefaced. Terrified. Deflated. Agitatedly, my wife said, "We just managed to escape by the skin of our teeth. There are some houses around the temple. In a split second, about a hundred people armed with lethal weapons surrounded us. They threatened to kill us if we shot at the bats. Do you know why? They believe that bats are the souls of our ancestors!"

I took a decision then. In no uncertain terms I said, "Bats are not the souls of our ancestors. But they are one among God's many creations. Let coconuts be destroyed. That doesn't matter. Let us be satisfied with what we get after they have taken their share. They certainly have a right to the coconuts. They too are part of the Almighty's creation, as are the palms. Remember the ancient right that God bequeathed at the auspicious moment of creation – *all* living beings are the rightful inheritors of the Earth."

This piece contains excerpts from "Bhoomiyute Avakasikal" (1977), first published in the anthology of the same name.

An evening prayer

At last, here I am, almighty God. Kneeling before you in supplication. In the desolation of this dark sphere.

O hidden God, is your abode beyond the galaxy of the shining stars, far beyond the reach of my imagination? Or are you close at hand – somewhere in this loneliness over which spreads the deepening dusk?

Creator of the universe, I want to resolve matters with you. But now, reduced to a bag of bones, and incapacitated in every way, I am ashamed to appear before you. You are omnipresent, while I am starving, homeless, with no raiments to cover my body. Legion are my companions in woe – lame, dumb, wasting away day by day. Is it possible that you do not hear our groans?

But that cannot be. The great gospels say that not even a blade of grass trembles without your consent or your knowledge. And you, Lord of all creation, can you forget your creatures? It seems so. For yugas now, you have quite forgotten us. The world has had no peace. Are our tears, cries, lamentations, bloodshed, wars, merely sources of entertainment for you?

The holy books and the preceptors do not speak of you as one indifferent and forgetful. You are known by a hundred names – all synonyms of your virtues. You are the compassionate one, the just one, the father of humankind. But, from time immemorial, men and women have appealed to you to assuage the hunger that gnaws at

translated by
Vanajam Ravindran

their bellies, to slake their thirst, to quench the more intense thirst of their hearts. And what have you done? The same prayers are still being uttered as we continue to suffer from pangs of hunger and unquenched thirst. What is the meaning of this? Are you a monster, blind and deaf?

You are called the Lord of Love – and you created disease, want and suffering? Are you really the just one – you who created the cruel, the arrogant, the tyrannical? Don't you expect us to bow before you? Didn't you create us because you wanted us to sing your praises?

You created us without our knowledge or consent. And long before we were born, you had already apportioned the bounties of the earth among the creatures who came ahead of us. That's you – the just one! You must understand that this seething mass of humanity are all your children. This world is a living death for us. And you talk of Heaven and Hell!

Let fires rain down from the firmament and burn us. Let your tempest and lightning strike at us. Unleash your great floods to drown us, one and all. No, that you will not do. You want to hear us sing the praises of our glorious God. If it is empty praises that you want to hear, listen. There is a voice from the church saying, "Come hither children of God, hasten to sing the praises of our Lord." From a distance I hear the muezzin's call summoning people to offer their obeisance to the Creator. And from the temple rises the resonant blowing of the conch. "Om Shantih, Shantih, Shantih." But what "Shantih" can you find in this babble, this cacophony?

Our eyes, blazing and fiery, betray but one emotion – indignation. Neither your beautiful Heaven nor your hideous Hell overwhelms us with desire or fear. Our hatred curls upwards in mounting flames ... Ah! I faint. I droop. I fall helpless before you, my God. Lead me to righteousness.

This piece was first published as "Sandhyapranamam" in the anthology entitled *Anarghanimisham* (1946).

Mantra Charatu

The mantra charatu appeared on the scene the day a mango fell with a thud on Abdul Aziz's bald pate. Ripe mangoes keep dropping from the tree near the courtyard. If not picked up immediately, you may be sure that Khan will snap them up, making them unfit for eating.

Khan, by the way, is Abdul Aziz's dog. A handsome chap, white with light brown spots, he gets the lion's share of the fallen mangoes and so everybody's main concern seems to be to save them from him. A strange dog, he is fond of jackfruit, banana and tea as well! He is always left free as he creates a racket if he is shut inside the house.

Recently, Khan has been lovelorn and languishing. He was in love with Malu, Parvathi's black bitch and the only good-looking one in the neighbourhood. It was a case of Hindu-Muslim romance. It was requited love too, and neither Parvathi nor Ummusalma, Abdul Aziz's wife, had any objection to their union. Why, Parvathi had even promised Ummusalma a pup from Malu sired by Khan.

Then fortune dealt a cruel blow. Six hefty dogs from somewhere suddenly appeared on the scene and started courting Malu. They seemed to resent the Khan-Malu union. In the encounter that followed, Khan's Hindu rivals almost reduced him to a pulp. Needless to say, Khan put up a brave fight, for his honour was at stake. A Muslim dog's spirited fight against kafirs! Snarling and ferocious, he held on to his rivals by the scruffs of their necks.

translated by
Vanajam Ravindran

The Hindu dogs vengefully lifted him off the ground and bit him so badly that he not only received deep gashes all over but also lost half of his right ear. Malu watched the gruesome battle with indifference. As did Parvathi and Ummusalma. This being a Hindu-Muslim conflict, they were at a loss as to whose side to take.

The vanquished Khan, blood streaming from his wounds, ran towards the kitchen and flopped on to the ground. But the Hindu dogs continued to challenge him by barking fiercely in unison. Khan, overcome by defeat, loss of face and the pain of thwarted love, held his peace. He could do nothing to counter the effects of his general debacle. All he felt was an intense aversion for the entire female species.

The first victims of Khan's rabid misogyny were two Hindu women. An anti-Hindu gesture, it was not a justifiable sentiment though. Since most of their neighbours were Hindus, either Ummusalma or Abdul Aziz were kept on the run, trying to escort the Hindu women visiting them, right from the gate to their doorstep.

The mango fell on Abdul Aziz's head when such was the state of affairs. At that very moment, the postman arrived. Khan fortunately felt no animosity towards Hindu men. The mango that hit Abdul Aziz's head was promptly presented to the postman. And as if in return, one of the letters Abdul Aziz received was from his bosom pal, Sankara Ayyar.

Abdul Aziz and Sankara Ayyar had been friends since their college days. Their bond was strengthened by a common affliction – baldness. And their one ambition was to see hair grow on their pates. They had taken recourse to all kinds of remedies and eagerly answered all advertisements guaranteeing a cure for baldness. They would share any and all information on this matter. Why, they even appealed to the powers above, making offerings to various deities!

Their respective spouses too played an active role in this project, massaging their husbands' heads with expensive medicinal oils and reminding the men to do so in their absence, among other things. But alas, all these were exercises in futility. The wives would sometimes laugh at the two eggheads who resembled each other so much. The little hair they had was at the back of their heads.

When Sankara Ayyar and Saraswathi recently visited them, the two women had counted the number of hair on the heads of their husbands. Saraswathi had conceded that Abdul Aziz had nine more than her husband. But then there was a reason for her favourable verdict on Aziz. During the early days of her pregnancy, he had constantly supplied her with the things she had craved for - raw mangoes, green tamarind and guavas.

Now, Aziz, who was reading his friend's letter, said with a hurt look, "Ummu, just see how Saraswathi retracts her statement. Does this mean that the woman lied blatantly for the sake of raw mangoes? You tell me, who has more hair, he or I?"

"You certainly are richer by nine hairs," Ummusalma reassured her husband. "Remember, we arrived at this verdict after much deliberation."

The offended Aziz, however, was unable to get over Saraswathi's duplicity. He remarked, "But now she is singing a different tune. This treachery, after all those mangoes ..."

Before he could complete the sentence, he heard someone at the gate greet him, "Asselamualaikkum!"

Abdul Aziz returned the greeting, "Va alaikkumusselam!"

Seeing the stranger, Ummusalma promptly went inside. The stranger, a tall, fair, venerable-looking man, was impeccably turned out in white trousers and a thin white kurta. He sported a white turban with a long fantail. His beard, sideburns and moustaches were so neatly trimmed that they looked unreal, his eyes were lined with surma. With him was a young boy clad in a shirt and dhoti, carrying a leather suitcase. The boy ceremoniously announced, "Sayinul Abideen Thangal!"

Thangal: The title denotes lineage from Prophet Mohammad.

PAUL KALLANODE

Abdul Aziz promptly offered a chair to the stranger. The boy respectfully deposited the box on another chair beside him.

"Is anyone unwell here?" Thangal asked.

Aziz reverentially replied, "No, at the moment no one is ill here."

"Are any wishes to be fulfilled?"

Who in this world is free from wishes? But what wishes were Abdul Aziz and Ummusalma harbouring in their hearts? No one knew.

When Thangal opened his box, it exuded the fragrance of attar. Inside the box were a number of black strings, each a foot long, paper tags attached to them.

"These are mantra charatus," he said. "Don't we invoke mantras on water and give it to people to cure their diseases? Don't we intercede on behalf of ill people and make offerings at various mosques and sacred tombs? No doubt one gets relief from all this, but it takes time to find a person who can chant the mantras and sometimes the right person may not be available. These charatus are very efficacious. I have imbued them with eternal, divine mantras."

Aziz picked up a thread and Thangal said, "That's for headaches – four rupees and ninety-five paise. All you need to do is tie it round your arm or neck and you will be free from headaches for the rest of your life. If it is covered by a sheath made of thin beaten gold or silver, the string won't get worn out either." Taking out the strings one by one, Thangal continued, "For cough, abdominal pain, heartburn, colic, toothache, hysteria, exorcising the devil, insanity, syphilis, leprosy, gonorrhoea, spinal problems, nightmares, worms, violent temper – four rupees ninety-five paise each."

Abdul Aziz asked naïvely, "Are these effective on animals as well?"

"Certainly, I've special ones for cows, goats, bullocks, horses and camels, even for fowls. If your hen doesn't lay eggs, all you have to do is tie a mantra charatu around one of its legs."

"Is there anything suitable for dogs? Our dog has now started biting Hindu women. Could you give us a mantra charatu which will stop him from doing so?"

"You mean a dog which bites only Hindu women?"

"Yes."

"Why is the dog averse to Hindu women alone?"

"Our dog was in love with Malu, the Hindu bitch that belongs to our neighbour Parvathi. But six hefty Hindu dogs tore him to shreds right in front of Malu and Parvathi. The poor chap lost half of his right ear too! You see, Parvathi stood watching the fight without as much as making an effort to stop it. That accounts for his resentment against Hindu women. But my wife Ummusalma too watched the fight as nonchalantly as Parvathi did. The dog ought to hate Muslim women as well."

"What is he called?"

"Khan."

The moment his name was mentioned, Khan presented himself before them.

"You see, he doesn't bite Muslim women precisely because he is called Khan," said Thangal profoundly.

Aziz repeated his question, "Do you have a charatu that will stop him from biting Hindu women?"

"I don't have one for just that purpose. But I do have a charatu which will prevent him from biting anyone. That should suffice – four rupees ninety-five paise only."

Thangal ran his eyes through the various labels and held out one. "Here it is. We must tie it round Khan's neck."

Abdul Aziz went inside to fetch a kindi of water and some soap. Thangal and Aziz stepped down to the courtyard. While the latter held Khan, Thangal tied the charatu round his neck. "According to Islam, anyone who touches a dog has to wash his hands seven times with mud," said Thangal.

As Abdul Aziz poured water, Thangal performed the ritual of washing his hands seven times with mud. Aziz did the same. After that they washed their hands with soap. Khan, with the black string around his neck and his one-and-a-half ears pricked up, stood there in great style. "From now on, he won't bite anybody because of the string's barkat," Thangal said.

Ummusalma appeared at the doorway with three glasses of tea. After drinking his tea, Thangal picked up a handful of strings and announced, "For deafness, weak eyesight, paralysis, rheumatic fever, lovesickness, for winning lotteries, promotion in jobs, diarrhoea, success in examinations, insomnia, for all uterine problems, infertility as well as getting rid of unwanted pregnancy, for getting a child of your choice, male or female, and for vanquishing your enemies. There's a charatu for every disease and every human problem. Each for four rupees ninety-five paise only."

"Will the potency of these diminish with time?" asked Aziz in all seriousness.

"Oh no! But with time the charatu may get worn out, which is why I advised you to have it sheathed in gold or silver. My father used to have one encased in silver. It is twenty years since Bapa died but I still use the charatu."

"Will the charatu meant for headache be equally effective for curing diarrhoea?" asked Aziz.

"Certainly not. You see, the charatus are of varying potency. For diarrhoea you have to use the one meant for that."

At this juncture, Ummusalma called her spouse inside. When he went up to her, she whispered in his ear, "Ask him if he has one to cure baldness."

"He may not," said Abdul Aziz in a hushed tone.

"Ask him anyway," Ummusalma insisted.

Abdul Aziz came out and said to Thangal, "Didn't you say you had charatus to counter all human problems? Do you have one which would cause hair to sprout on a bald head?"

Aziz was pleasantly surprised when Thangal pulled out a bundle of strings from the bottom of his box. The label on each said, "For Baldness."

"You will have to tie it round your waist."

"Then I'll have to join it with another. I have a friend, Sankara Ayyar, who is bald like me. If it is to be tied round the waist I will need four strings in all. Two for me and two for him."

Thangal himself joined the strings for Abdul Aziz.

Aziz took it to Ummusalma who solemnly tied it round her spouse's waist. He felt a strange sensation pass through his head and body. The charatus meant for Sankara Ayyar were put in a large envelope with a brief letter mentioning their efficacy. He handed to Thangal twenty-four rupees and seventy-five paise, the net price for five mantra charatus – Khan's, Sankara Ayyar's and his.

Aziz enthused, "This secret miracle should be brought to the notice of our government. Crores of rupees are being spent on hospitals, medicines and doctors. A criminal waste indeed! Were we to make these charatus available everywhere, hospitals could be converted to five star hotels or other useful things. The charatus should be available at groceries, cigarette shops, bus stands, railway stations and airports. You can have a special department to look after the distribution of this essential commodity. Why, it could become an export item. You will find a good market in England, Germany, Japan, America and Russia where the expenditure on hospitals and medicines is prohibitive. And, in the bargain, you can make some money too."

"But who should I get in touch with for implementing this scheme?"

"You need only see our Prime Minister."

"That should be possible, I think. Aren't there some Muslim ministers? They would certainly help me," agreed Thangal.

"In your esteemed opinion, how are diseases caused?" Aziz asked.

"They are all the evil doings of Shaitan and the djinns. Take the case of baldness. What do you think is the cause?"

"Falling hair," said Abdul Aziz.

"And why does hair fall?"

"I don't know."

"Then let me tell you. The evil spirits pull out your hair. They live on the moon."

"But as far as I know the moon has no inhabitants. The newspapers said so after the scientists landed there."

"Don't you believe them! It is impossible to reach the moon. What they claim to have brought back from there were all picked up from some hillock on earth. No, they can't reach the moon and they won't," said Thangal emphatically.

Thangal and the boy were ready to depart. While taking leave he said, "I shall try to meet the Prime Minister through some Muslim ministers, for promoting these charatus. Asselamualaikkum!"

"Va alaikkumusselam!"

That very day the mantra charatus, along with a letter, were mailed to Sankara Ayyar by registered post. One week passed.

Around this time, Lalitha, a pretty Hindu girl, who had come to Abdul Aziz's place on an important errand, was bitten by Khan. The bite was not a deep one, only some teeth marks were left on Lalitha's thigh. Ummusalma applied a herbal remedy made from bitter gourd on them. She also mended the tear in Lalitha's saree and, after giving her some tea, lent her the twenty-five rupees she had come to borrow.

Strange, Khan's animosity towards Hindu women had not abated despite the charatu. But his latest act was a mere vestige of his earlier aversion. No, you really couldn't call it a bite. By and by, his urge to bite will pass off, they said.

But what about the hair that was supposed to grow on Abdul Aziz's head? Daily, Ummusalma would intently look for any sign of sprouting hair as she massaged her husband's head.

A month passed. There was no visible improvement. Then, a terrible thing happened. Khan now hated Muslim women as well. It was very evident that he had turned a complete misogynist.

When Ummusalma's mother came to visit them, Khan bit her.

"Rabbe," she shouted. "Save me, your dog will finish me off. Kill that creature!"

Panicking, Ummusalma and Abdul Aziz rushed towards her to find Khan innocently standing there, the charatu hanging round his neck.

But why should poor Khan, whose strange behaviour is the result of frustration in love, be killed? These days he generally dislikes women, but so far he has not vented his wrath on Ummusalma. But her mother? The thought tickled Abdul Aziz, who was mentally savouring various methods of torturing his mother-in-law. Though pleased with what Khan had done, he made a pretence of punishing him by muzzling and shutting him in a room. He then washed his hands seven times with mud. Ummusalma, after the ritual cleaning of her mother's wound, administered her customary herbal remedy.

Time passed and nothing significant happened as far as Abdul Aziz's baldness was concerned – it was the same shining pate. "Has anything happened to Sankara Ayyar's head?" wondered Aziz. Maybe the mantra charatu was ineffective. Khan continued to bite women. Could it be that all his sprouting hair was being pulled out by djinns? But why would they need human hair? Surely there must be mantra charatus to keep the djinns in their place. Perhaps there were other charatus potent enough to counter the effect of those given by Thangal. But what parties would be interested in making Thangal's charatus counterproductive? Why, all those associated with the medical profession and drug manufacturers! Had more charatus come into the market? These were the thoughts that passed through Aziz's mind. Altogether, it seemed a knotty problem, totally beyond his powers of comprehension. But then who could he ask for advice?

Abdul Aziz and Ummusalma, after reviewing the situation, wondered whether they should continue to use the charatus. A final decision was taken. Aziz snipped off Khan's string with a pair of scissors. With the same pair of scissors, Ummusalma cut the charatus around her husband's waist. The discarded strings were then taken to the courtyard, doused in kerosene and burned. Nothing spectacular happened. No explosion! The charred threads, soon reduced to ashes, were picked up and buried under the mango tree.

A great burden seemed to be off their minds. But, lo and behold! An urgent letter arrived from Sankara Ayyar, accompanied by a money order for a hundred rupees. The letter carried news of vital importance. Sankara Ayyar was ecstatic. He wrote:

> Many thanks for the charatu. The day I wore it around my waist, I purchased a one rupee lottery ticket which won a prize of thousand rupees! The same thread was later tied round Saraswathi's waist. The result? Easy delivery ... a baby boy! This was all because of the miraculous charatu! Please get me as many of them as you can with the money I am sending. My parents want one each, so do I, and we need one for the baby. If this money is not enough I shall send you more ...

However, there was no mention of hair on his bald head.

"Mantra charatu" was first published in the anthology *Anappoota* (1975).

PAUL KALLANODE

Voices

THE MIDNIGHT VISITOR

"Once upon a time, there was a young man who did not know who his parents were. He had committed many murders. At the age of twenty-four, he ..."

"May I interrupt you? Are you about to begin the story?"

"Yes."

"Who are you talking about?"

"Myself."

"Not bad for a beginning!"

"Didn't you say that I could begin the story at any point?"

"Yes. But I didn't mean it. I thought you were ..."

"Mad, right?"

"What's wrong with you?"

"I'm mad."

"So? There is a streak of madness in all of us, though in varying degrees. But that is no reason not to brush your teeth and wash yourself, is it? Look at your hair, your beard, your stinking clothes – your whole appearance! Why can't you at least take a bath and look clean?"

"I consider water to be the blood of the earth. And ..."

"And?"

"I don't have any clean clothes to change into. No towel either."

"Who sent you here at this unearthly hour?"

"No one. I had seen you during the day. I heard your name being mentioned and people pointing you out. So I

translated by
V C Harris

followed you. Others joined you on the way. Then all of you congregated in this room, and talked, laughed and argued noisily. When I saw them leave, I came in."

"So you have been waiting in the dark pathway till now?"

"Yes."

"But how do you know me?"

"I have read your books."

"Where did you find them?"

"I bought them."

"Where did you get the money for that?"

"I was in the army."

"Is that how you became a murderer?"

"Yes. And it was not just my enemies that I killed. Enemies. Friends. Do these words mean anything?"

"So you are one of my fans?"

"Yes."

"Have you brought anything for me?"

"No."

"Why are you here?"

"What do you think of murder?"

"You mean, is it right or wrong? What can I say?"

"You have no views on the matter?"

"Don't be angry. I will say something. I don't like the idea of getting killed. What I normally do is this. I see if my enemy is stronger than me. If he isn't, I valiantly oppose him. If not, I beat a hasty retreat."

"Are you making fun of me?"

"What do you want from me?"

"I have no philosophy of life. I just want to tell you about some of my experiences."

"Couldn't you do it tomorrow? I am tired of listening to people. I want to eat and go to sleep. You may come tomorrow, but not too early. Around eleven or twelve. I get up very late."

"Where do I stay till then?"

"Isn't there anywhere you can go?"

"No."

"No acquaintances?"

"Acquaintances? In this world?"

"Have you eaten anything?"

"No."

"Do you have any money?"

"No."

"Oh my god!"

"What do you intend to do now?"

"Intend?"

"Yes."

"One, don't lose your temper. Two, don't glare at me. Three, go brush your teeth and have a bath. Four, use the fresh clothes that I give you. Five, if you want to brush your hair and beard, I have no comb to offer you. Six, there is food for one person, we will share it. Agreed?"

"Agreed."

"Well, go that way to the other room without touching my bed. Pick up a towel, take some tooth powder from the paper packet that is kept in the corner. The torch too. That is the bathroom. Go and have a wash. No, wait a moment. I will give you some clean clothes. Don't bring back the ones you are wearing now. Your bed is in the other room. When I go to sleep, I will lock this door. You can use the other room as yours. You are free to come and go as you like. Now, wash and then we will eat whatever there is and go to sleep. Everything else can be taken care of tomorrow. All right?"

"All right."

"By the way, were you discharged from the army?"

"Yes. Why do you ask? Didn't you know? We won the war."

"How many were discharged?"

"About four-five million."

"Are you their representative?"

"I don't represent anyone but myself. Don't I have the right to express my own views?"

"Certainly."

"I have no particular attachment to anything. I love the earth, the whole universe. I was born in this world, so everyone here is related to me – all those who profess different views, different religions – I love them all. I became a soldier. What is a soldier's duty? Kill as many people as you can! And I killed, so that a few vile despicable creatures could rule over this country. I am referring to leaders the world over. Not one of them was on the battlefield, nor their kith and kin. People armed with lethal weapons destroyed one another. A people's war indeed! Which people, I ask you?"

"Didn't I tell you not to lose your temper? I didn't send you to the army. So why should you vent your spleen on me?"

"I have to vent it on someone. I have been deeply hurt."

"Great!"

"Now what?"

"Be calm. Go wash. We will eat and go to sleep."

AT THE CROSSROADS

"For days now, I have not slept in peace. How could I when I didn't have a home, a job, or food to eat?"

"Don't you know your parents?"

"No."

"Then how were you ..."

"Born? Like all of you, like all human beings on earth!"

"But I have parents. And brothers and sisters too."

"I have no one."

"Where were you born?"

"Where four roads meet."

"You mean ..."

"All I know is what my foster father told me before he died. He found me early one morning, abandoned on the wayside. A newborn babe. Swaddled in rags. Left alone in the dark."

"What happened then?"

"He picked me up. Informed the police. Informed the authorities."

"Then?"

"What could they do? Nobody wanted me. So he took charge of me. I squalled terribly when he washed me. He wrapped me in a clean white cloth. Gave me a name. A name from among millions of other names. I was brought up in accordance with his religion. He also gave me a decent education."

"So you grew up as one belonging to his community?"

"Yes, except that I don't believe in any religion now. All religions are more or less the same. They try to make us better human beings."

"Which religion were you born into?"

"How do you expect me to know that? I could have been anything. Christian, Muslim, Hindu, Jewish, Parsi, Jain, Buddhist, Sikh. Or perhaps a cross. Whatever I was, the fact remains that I have never suckled at a mother's breast. Whenever I see a woman's breasts I feel a great thirst. Breasts, breasts, so many of them!"

"What did you do after your foster father died?"

"Gave up my studies and started looking for a job. Finally, I became a soldier. I can't tell you the story of my life in any sequential or chronological order. I can only tell you things at random."

"What did your foster father do?"

"He was a priest. A pujari in a temple. An old man who had no close relatives. He was a very kind and god-fearing man. Can I ask you something: Does God exist?"

"Yes, If you want Him to exist."

"Why do you say that?"

"Well, that is how I feel now in this thirty-fourth year of my life. God is the merciful one who created you, me and the whole universe, isn't he? The universe does not exist or collapse on the basis of our faith or belief. You may choose to believe in Him or not. What matters is one's sense of contentment. How old are you?"

"Twenty-nine."

"Haven't you ever felt the urge to find out who your parents were?"

"I made enquiries. Over and over again. My foster father and I came here and asked a lot of people."

"Here?"

"Yes. It was at the crossroads here that I was found."

"I see. Anyhow, yours is not a unique story. You weren't strangled to death and thrown away for some street dog to eat, were you? You owe your existence to an unknown woman's kindness. You are the living image of that kindness."

"What are you sketching?"

"I am not sketching. I'm writing. I am not a tape recorder, right? Sooner or later I will forget what you tell me. After all, it isn't my own experience. So I am taking down everything while it is still fresh in my mind. I will read it out to you later. There will be nothing here that you didn't tell me. Is that all right?"

"Yes."

THE BLOOD OF THE EARTH

"Why do you think that water is the blood of the earth?"

"As I said, I have killed so many people. Why, every soldier is a potential killer! Even now there must be a war going on in some corner of the earth. Who is responsible for that?"

"Who do you think is responsible?"

"Emperors, presidents, dictators – aren't they all murderers?"

"Are they?"

"Yes, they are. Their estates are soaked in human blood. And they drink the people's blood. They ..."

"Wait a minute, let me ask you something: In a war isn't one side always in the wrong?"

"What if you look at it from the point of view of the other side?"

"You can't live if you go on looking at things from the other perspective, can you? From the point of view of animals, birds and fish, trees and other living things, all human beings are murderers. What have you to say to that?"

"Is that a good answer? Anyway, let me now tell you my love story."

"What about the earth's blood?"

"I don't want to talk about it."

"Why?"

"I will tell you about someone I killed."

"First tell me about the earth's blood. Why do you think that way?"

"I can't explain it ... It is difficult to recall every single detail. One night, after a day-long battle, about five hundred of us drank some water. In the morning we saw that what remained in the vessel was blood. The field was strewn with dead bodies. Many of them were mutilated beyond recognition.

Now I will tell you about the other matter. It is still clear in my mind – the death of a friend. It was I who killed him. I fired at him twice or thrice in broad daylight. It was summer. The heat was unbearable. The battlefield reverberated with deafening explosions. Bombs exploded with a blinding light. Bullets whizzed past. The roaring of the warplanes continued. Heat. Sweat. Panic. Wailing. Destruction. At the end of the day, an uneasy and unnatural calm prevailed.

We spent the days and nights moving, eating and sleeping, as if in a dream. Once I found a human eye in my food. Mutilated bodies lay all around. Stinking, decaying corpses. Death was everywhere. I don't know why I didn't die. This is not my experience alone. Every soldier will tell you the same story.

As I stood there with my friend, a bomb exploded about forty feet away and I was almost buried under the rubble thrown out from the crater it caused. It was noon. My eyes, nose and mouth were filled with mud. Somehow I crawled out. A fire raged on all sides. I could hear the flames crackle. Then I heard my friend's agonized cry. Groaning in pain, he lay beside me. The bomb had not killed him. He said, Kill me, in the name of God kill me. Please, I can't bear it.

I will not be able to forget the sight till I die. Imagine your skin frazzled from the soles of your feet to the top of your head, blood oozing out all over the body. At first, I thought he was on fire – a naked, burning, blood-red man. Those eyes! Blood dripped from his fingers, from his penis. Drip, drip, drip. It dripped on to the uniform of a dead soldier."

THE BELOVED

"Tell me your love story now."

"All soldiers have their sweethearts. One is often shared by many, or sometimes there are many women for a single person. It's all very confusing. Ordinary soldiers usually end up with cheap prostitutes. As your rank rises, the social status of the women you get also goes up. What do you have to say about prostitution?"

"You mean, whether it is right or wrong?"

"Yes."

"I have heard that prostitution is the oldest profession in the world. And that it is practised even today – by beggars and by queens. But I wouldn't like my mother or wife or sisters to be prostitutes."

"Do you have a wife?"

"Legally wedded? No."

"Otherwise?"

"Let us assume that I don't have one. Even if I did, I wouldn't like her to be a prostitute. Well, get on with your story."

"Did you ever feel that prostitution is always the result of an economic problem?"

"Must be."

"Why do women turn to it?"

"Perhaps because there are a lot of men around."

"Is that a good answer?"

"Why do men go to them? Let us not waste time in pointless arguments. From the man's point of view it is always the woman's fault. Women feel that it is men who are responsible. Either both parties are to blame, or neither. On what basis can you possibly pass judgement on what is right or wrong?"

"On the basis of morality."

"Whose sense of morality? Of which part of the world, what people?"

"I wouldn't know. Isn't there something loosely called morality? Like abstaining from promiscuous sex, observing chastity and so on?"

"Each religion has its own moral codes. Take monogamy, for instance. Some religions allow polygamy and some polyandry. There are some communities in which both the royalty and the common folk can marry their own mothers and sisters. That is their idea of morality. And haven't you heard of things like phallus worship, yoni puja, and so on? What's the moral code in these cases? Why, it's the same practice as among animals, birds and reptiles."

"But isn't that horrible?"

"Why do you think so?"

"I ... I don't know."

"I will tell you. You have a certain philosophy of life. To say that you don't is not correct. You have always had it, right from your childhood. Your foster father was a priest, wasn't he? He taught you about good and evil. And that moral sense is your philosophy of life."

"Perhaps you are right. Let me ask you something: Is it possible to maintain honesty in a man-woman relationship?"

"In sexual matters, you mean?"

"Yes."

"You can't expect me to speak for all the people in the world. On my part, I wish such honesty were possible. But in general, is anyone consistently honest? We try to appear honest to others, but are we really honest? Our days, our nights ..."

"What do you think of the future of humankind?"

"It is not too bleak. Why do you ask?"

"These days, seven out of ten people suffer from gonorrhoea or syphilis."

"Who told you this?"

"A respected army doctor."

"Perhaps he was trying to frighten you people?"

"In the army, nine out of ten men contract these diseases. This is a fact. They constantly live in the shadow of death. As for civilians, I am talking of beggars, labourers, bureaucrats, lawyers, politicians, actors, celibate priests, journalists, writers, prostitutes, presidents – most of them too are victims of these diseases."

"I don't know this for a fact. But such diseases can be cured with potent medicines."

"The medicines are very expensive, and only the rich can afford them. Moreover the diseases are not completely curable. They are like smouldering embers hidden in ashes. Doctors say that gonorrhoea has been known to be transmitted through three generations. Through blood and semen. I don't know if it is more terrible than leprosy, but I am scared to visit prostitutes. I have never gone to them. I had sexual intercourse only after being discharged from military service. This was when I was living in a city. Till then, that is as long as I remained in the army, my sweetheart was the photograph of a film actress. And that snap was the sweetheart of almost all of us who were unmarried."

"What do you mean?"

"The photograph had lips, eyes, breasts, navel, thighs. And we had imagination. Kissing, embracing, making love ..."

"I see."

"Just think of our lives! We who live in this world ... of all that transpires in our bedrooms ..."

"Aren't there millions of men and women in this world including you and me? What is so significant about bedrooms? We are all creatures of flesh and blood, desires and longings. Let me hear the story of how you became a lover."

THE LOVER

"I became a lover when I was staying in the house of an important person in the city. This was immediately after I was discharged from the army, when demobbed soldiers roamed about the streets looking for jobs. There was famine and epidemic all around. But that is not unusual, I suppose. Whatever may happen, for a man to live without a woman that long, without having sexual relationships ...”

“Wait a minute, please. How did you land in that prominent person's bungalow?”

“Communal or political, I don't know which, but there was a riot. A people's riot! I was watching it from the top floor of a hotel. There was a beautiful sunset. But the sun had not completely set. Let me ask you something: Is there an end to such conflicts in this world?”

“As long as there is more than one person or more than one opinion ...”

“But who is right?”

“It is up to you to decide. You have a head and brains. Think. If you can't do it, accept whichever view seems most convincing.”

“What do all these opinions mean?”

“I don't understand your question.”

“There are so many religions. And political organizations. All of them are clamouring for supremacy. Killing people. What do they want?”

“Power.”

“But to what purpose?”

“To rule over every human being and living creature on this earth. Religions are propagated in the name of God to this end. And if you are an unbeliever, you wield power in your own name.”

“Meaning?”

“Each person wants to govern according to his own scheme of things.”

“But I don't have a philosophy of life. Is it because I have nobody in this world to call my own?”

“You do have a philosophy, as I told you earlier. And talking of relationships, you have a certain relationship with everyone.”

“What relationship?”

"Don't you have a navel?"

"Navel? What about it?"

"Through it, you are bound to your unknown mother."

"So what?"

"Your unknown father is bound to his mother and so on. In short, everyone in this world is related to one another."

"Perhaps. But I don't feel anything binding about it."

"All right then, we're wasting our time talking about this and that. Tell me about the story of your love. You said you were standing on the top floor of the city hotel, and that it was a beautiful sunset ..."

"The sun hadn't set. Imagine the city as a huge forest infested with predatory animals. Imagine the city growling, snarling, roaring. The deafening sound of speeding vehicles, a seething mass of humanity racing in different directions. Tall buildings almost touching the sky – hospitals, hotels, offices, liquor shops and factories. Each sporting its own bit of cloth."

"What cloth?"

"Multi-coloured flags, each a symbol of a party."

"I see."

"Every such bit of painted cloth is a sign of the people, isn't it?"

"Yes."

"The flag bearers ... all of them subscribe to their own party agenda, don't they?"

"Yes."

"All of them address people's issues, don't they?"

"Yes, members of different parties say different things."

"A godown full of explosives belonging to a certain group caught fire. A procession taken out by one group clashed with a rival group. And then there was a rain of hand bombs, stones and broken soda bottles. Knives were thrust into human hearts. Slogans were followed by counter slogans. The entire thing was a bloodbath, a dance of death. The police arrived and then the army. Tat-tat-tat went the rattling machine guns, playing havoc. An aircraft hovered over the city, whirring, screeching and tearing away. The smell of blood and gunpowder spread as the hot wind blew.

And then, like every other day, the city lights appeared. Full-throated songs of love and desire blared out from the cinemas. Advertisements in garish neon lights glittered above the tall buildings. What a terrible, wonderful city! Six-storeyed buildings were catching fire like heaps of dry leaves. And those flames were reflected in a thousand eyes. People were charred to ashes. The wailing of fire engines could be heard every once in while. Along with the clanging of bells. Somewhere, a huge pipe burst with a terrible sound, spouting a jet of water into the sky.

The hotel where I was staying was gutted. Panic-stricken people, blinded and choked by smoke, started rushing out. So did I. My clothes were ablaze as I ran frantically. Later, the prominent person I referred to earlier, said that I had rescued a number of people from the hotel. I don't know ... I can't remember anything.

When I came to, I was in his bungalow. His wife, children and everybody else there liked me. I was a hero. The pride of my country! The country needed more young men like me! I think he got my photograph published in some newspaper along with a statement. More statements followed in the wake of the first one in the next few days. Statements issued by leaders. Counter statements. Lots of people had died, people affiliated to different flags. And then the statistics of death. Rotten lies. The flag wavers, they uttered those lies, published them in newspapers, made umpteen speeches. Those people were all the same. Only the slogans were different. The brotherhood of explosive bombs and the many-hued flags."

"What about your becoming a lover?"

"I am coming to it. I stayed on in that important man's house. The garage there had a room on either side. One for me, the other for the driver. I had my meals in the room. I had total freedom, almost like a member of the family. One evening, as I sat in my room, the city suddenly came alive with lights. At that very moment I became a lover."

THE IMAGE OF LOVE

"A dreamy-eyed smile. Firm shapely breasts. That gait! That look! Every evening she would walk past my room. She would look at me and smile. I too would try to smile, but did not have the courage to do so. She didn't know who I was. Perhaps she thought I was a member of that prominent family. Once she knew who and what I really was, perhaps everything would change. But who was she? A student or a working woman? Whoever she was, to me she was a sweet poem finely chiselled in loveliness! I knew not her name, yet she held my heart captive, unleashing a storm in my life.

How I longed for a kiss, a passionate embrace. How did a woman look without her clothes? I didn't know. But I wanted to know. I longed to see her undressed. To touch her, kiss her, hold her tight. O, the smell of woman! I lived in a state of desire so intense that it could pulverize even granite. I would stand at the window, looking at the crowded street with great expectation. She would appear every evening the moment the street lights were turned on. Each day her dress would be of a different colour with a matching handbag and footwear.

Then, one evening, the lights came on. The city whirred louder. My heart thumped faster. There she was! A glance full of love! Then she moved on. I locked my room and stepped out into the street. She saw me and slowed down. I drew near. She looked at me with a lovely, endearing smile. Then she asked me in a voice that suggested a bad throat, sweet but husky: Where are you going?

I attempted a smile in reply. Where could I go! I began to sweat. My mouth turned dry. A whiff of heady perfume hit my nostrils. Her face was as fair as jasmine, her lips were red like roses, her hair black as night. I wanted to kiss her all over. Her lovely breasts could be seen through her thin blouse. She clutched a parasol and a handbag in her left hand. In the right, she held a handkerchief.

Aching with love and desire, I walked by her side. I could not make much conversation. Just then, a motor car came racing towards us and I saw my host's wife in it. I withdrew into the shadows to avoid being seen. The car passed by. I was alone. But at my feet lay the handkerchief. It had touched her face, her lips and sweat. I picked it up and kissed it a thousand times and kept it under my shirt, close to my heart."

THE SCENTED HANDKERCHIEF

"And then?"

"I am telling you. Look there, above that tree there."

"The moonlight?"

"What a wonderfully perfect circle! Like glowing white powder, like a hazy, heatless day. Why is the moonlight so ... Look at the green foliage shimmering, shimmering. On the mountains and deserts and oceans ..."

"The moonlight can wait. What about the scented handkerchief?"

"Have you ever received a gift of love?"

"Plenty."

"What value would it have for you?"

"Why do you ask?"

"Well, I just asked."

"Love is not a new emotion after all. Look at the moon. Ages and ages ago, ever since human beings appeared on this earth, that strange something that man feels towards woman has been compared with the moon ... What I'm trying to say is that love is a very, very old notion. Man has loved woman, and woman man, from time immemorial. The mutual attraction of male and female exists among all living creatures. Mating. Multiplying. Loving. A wonderful confidence trick with a little perfume sprayed over!"

"Yes, it's all quite wonderful."

"The living creatures, the earth and the moon and the stars ..."

"I am thinking of that perfumed handkerchief. Do you know how many times I kissed it that night? And the dreams that I had! My love overflowed the bungalow, the city!"

"What did you do in that house?"

"Nothing much. I taught the children there. Four or five of them. Actually, I looked after them."

"Did the people of the house know everything about you?"

"Certain things, yes. All of them loved me. Human beings are such wonderful creatures!"

"No doubts about it. You are a wonderful creature yourself!"

"Sometimes, I feel very sad. Let's say, it is a sorrow blended with the sweetness of poetry. On moonlit nights, I feel like that. What about you?"

"I don't know. Perhaps all living creatures feel so at times."

"Are there living beings on the moon?"

"Scientists say there aren't. The moon is supposed to be a dead world."

"And the stars?"

"They say some of the stars might have living things on them. A long time from now, that is, in the distant future, who knows what might happen? In the primeval days there was nothing!"

"Nothing?"

"Nothing. No earth, moon, sun, nor stars. The great, great wondrous universe is truly beyond our intelligence!"

"Then where did it all come from?"

"God created it from nothing. But unbelievers say that the universe and the earth and human beings evolved by themselves."

"Which view is right?"

"What can I say? In some scriptures, the earth is said to be flat. In others, the universe consists only of the earth, the sun, the moon and a few stars. Some others mention the earth as a goddess, the sun and the moon as gods. There are those who believe that this globe is merely a large lump of earth. A few religions and most scientists hold that the earth is round. Who is right? But you don't believe in any religion, do you? So you are free to believe in whatever sounds right."

"Some scriptures describe the sun, the moon and the stars as lamps lit by God. What do you think, how did man come into being?"

"Why man alone? Aren't there other living beings as well? How did they all come into being? You can think about it yourself and reach your own conclusions. In other words, I know nothing. I've heard scientists speak of it. But they all have different views. Let me tell you the gist of it. It's nothing new, though. Take your imagination back to the origins of the universe. A billion years. Look, here you go, ten years, a hundred years, a thousand years, before you and I were born, before the human race came into being, before the living creatures on earth came into being, before the earth and the waters were created. Millions of years ago ... Imagine the earth as a burning, red-hot ball of fire that turned round and round ... Prior to that, this ball of fire was a mere drop in the vast burning spaces of the melting sun ... This flaming droplet was thrown out into the universe, only to go round and round in an orbit, turning through many days and nights. No, there were no days and nights then ... The ball kept burning, burning."

"And then?"

"Then it cooled down and solidified. Ages went by. Water and earth, rivers and lakes and reptiles, weeds, plants and trees came into being. Then came birds and animals. Ages passed. Those prehistoric times came to an end. Human beings appeared – primitive men and women. Life moved on through days and nights of endless time.

There may be a few errors here and there in my account but this is the gist of the matter. Of all living beings only humans progressed right through the years. Hunting and dwelling in caves, cultivating land and settling in groups, then establishing religions, places of worship, towns, cities, machines, automobiles – thus goes the story of the human race. And it goes on endlessly."

"What about the future?"

"Of the human race?"

"Yes."

"Beautiful, promising. That's how we should think of it. Though there are terrible diseases around, we have medicines too. Then there are weapons, machines, electricity. Vehicles that ply on the surface of the earth, those that fly through the sky, those that move along the surface of the water and beneath. Spacecrafts, satellites!"

"What is inside the earth?"

"The stuff that flows out when volcanoes erupt – molten metals, minerals. Inside the earth, there must be something that burns and melts in the terrible heat – iron or matter of that kind."

"Will the earth too ultimately become a dead world?"

"That you and I will no longer be around after a while is true. Why should we think about the future of the earth and the universe?"

"Hasn't it been said that the moon is a dead world?"

"No one knows whether there was anything in the past. Why should we rack our brains with thoughts that we can't make head or tail of? Let's assume that everything was created by God, that the sun and moon and stars are lamps lit for us by God in his compassion."

"In that case one will have to believe in religions, in heaven and hell."

"Believe – who says you shouldn't?"

"Do you believe in them?"

"What I believe is ... but why should I tell you?"

"Just like that."

"No. You too live on this earth. Think about it and reach your own conclusions. We're still wasting our time talking about unnecessary things. Tell me what you have to. I have to get back to my writing."

"Where did I stop?"

"The scented handkerchief. Then you saw the glowing moon ... Yes, and you kissed the handkerchief, and dreamt ..."

"That is right. It was perfumed, with the most expensive perfume on earth! My host's wife used the same kind of thing. It was the maid who gave me this information. I was carrying that handkerchief with the divine fragrance in my pocket. When she brought me coffee and snacks, the maid said, Master, you smell like our madam! I didn't pay attention to her chatter. I kept thinking of my beloved."

"And then?"

"There was a wedding. My host's daughter's. A feast. Fireworks. All the local worthies were there. Guests were served whatever they wanted - unlimited liquor, everything. By evening I was quite drunk. My beloved appeared. And I went with her. She hired a taxi."

"And then?"

"She gave me a dreamy-eyed smile. She took me to her room and locked the door, embraced me and seated me on her bed. The room was drowned in darkness. Divine fragrance. I kissed her on her face, her eyes. Kissed her many times on her lovely breasts. We were locked in a passionate embrace.

I ... I was like a river gushing from a mountain spring. The mountain that had been obstructing my flow for ages suddenly seemed to break into fragments, and I was rushing forward at a terrific pace, and losing myself in the vast, boundless ocean. I emerged from the ocean of ecstasy and opened my eyes. The lights came on again. My head had cleared. I felt very fulfilled. The contentment of ages.

·But the surroundings were rather unwholesome. The plaster was peeling off, the walls looked as if they were afflicted with sores. Stinking clothes were heaped on a line against a wall. The whole room was filled with a foul odour mingled with fragrance.

Do you want anything to drink? I was startled. What kind of a voice was this - raucous like a crow's, not one bit of femininity in it. Black hair peeked out from under her blouse. I was shocked, scared, disgusted. I rose to my feet and held her breasts. They were mere pads of cotton wool. I just sat there. Many hours must have passed, or perhaps only a few minutes. I uncovered the bosom. A man's hairy chest! I placed the artificial breasts attached to the blouse on the bed. Lovely breasts indeed! I don't know what I felt at the moment - anger, surprise, sorrow, disgust or fear. I lit a cigarette and blew out the smoke. Smoke - a life that goes up in smoke! I could hear the sound of fireworks rising above the din of the city. I asked, You were born a man and yet?"

THE MALE PROSTITUTE

"She ... it ... he came to me, picked his artificial breasts, tied them on, and then went on to wear the saree daintily. He asked, Have you never seen people like me? I said, People like you? And he said, They can be found everywhere.

Later I came to know that in the past, in the palaces of emperors, you could always find such eunuchs. Were all transvestites like this? I stood and stared, I who had not known any woman, never seen one without her clothes on. What had I done under the spell of love, lust and liquor? I broke out into a sweat. I seemed to burn. What had I done? I was filled with sympathy and anger, fear, disgust and hatred.

I asked, How many people are like you in this place? He replied, Lots. I wanted to know, How did you become like this? He turned his face away. I persisted. Painting his lips red, he said, We have a group, a society. Not one, in fact there are many. Of hijras or hermaphrodites. People from different beliefs and faiths. Before you can join a group, you have to go through an initiation ceremony. You will be stripped and seated on a sharp spike, something like a nilavilakku. You will have to undergo a very painful surgery, losing a lot of blood. Then there is a marriage ceremony, attended by everyone in the group. After a lot of singing and dancing, the hair on your face is plucked off and you are given a woman's name. Then you wear a saree, a skirt and these artificial breasts ... and grow your hair long like a woman's.

What kind of people approach you? I asked.

To which he said, Both men and women. Then I asked, Can you ... like a man? His reply was, No. So I asked, Then why do women come to you? He said, Don't you know why? We can give them pleasure.

Tell me your story, I pleaded. He said, I have no story to tell. I continued, About your childhood then, don't you have parents? Yes, he said, They are far away. They don't know that I'm like this. I have stayed in the house where you are now. Today is his daughter's

---

Nilavilakku: The traditional oil lamp on a stand, usually of bronze or silver.

wedding, isn't it? Yes, I said. He told me, That girl's mother used to be very fond of me! Then I said, I have no father or mother or anyone. I was a baby discarded at the crossroads, wrapped in rags.

He did not believe me, but he narrated his story to me. His teacher, his classmates – they were all part of the story. He was born in a village about fifty miles from the city. When he was fourteen his male teacher sexually abused him. Teacher, yes! Excellent! A person who was supposed to teach him morals and manners even introduced the boy to the pleasures of masturbation! And soon he learned all the sexual perversions prevalent in schools, colleges, convents and monasteries. At sixteen he became an attendant in a hotel. And there he contracted gonorrhoea from a colleague. All attendants have either gonorrhoea or syphilis.

He left the town and after wandering around for some time, drifted to the city. He stayed with my host's driver for a while and then moved into the bungalow. At first he was just a servant, later he was required to massage my host – his legs, thighs and upwards. And the mistress of the house wanted more than that! At that time he was not a fully-grown male. At last he became an acknowledged male prostitute. That street belonged to people like him. They would visit the rich people's houses, singing, dancing, beating drums. There were quite a lot of them – the same number as female prostitutes. And I caught syphilis and gonorrhoea from him."

"You?"

"Yes."

"Are you infected even now?"

"Yes. I thought you had already realized it."

"Why?"

"Your instructions about the towel and the bed."

"O, that is because I don't usually allow other people to use my things. A towel used by someone else to wipe his arse clean, a sheet that bears someone else's sweat. People have all kinds of diseases ... infectious diseases, you know. And I do have all kinds of people calling on me at odd hours. So I keep an extra bed and a towel ready in the other room, that's all."

"I thought otherwise."

"Is it infectious?"

"Yes, you can contract it through bedclothes and towels. Even through sweat."

"Good that you spent all your time in that room."

"I am now going to tell you the story of a mother and son."

"How did you happen to leave your host's bungalow?"

"I was ill. I could not look them in the face. So I left. No food. No money for treatment. Nowhere to stay. It was when I was wandering thus that I saw the mother and her son. She kicked me on my chest."

"Wait a minute. What did the male prostitute say in the end?"

"He looked at me with unsatisfied desire and said, You know how my heart thirsts when I meet a strong and handsome man. I came away, saying I would go back the next day. He took all my money."

"That's how you ...?"

"Yes."

"Is it very painful?"

"It's impossible to urinate. You feel like emptying out a whole sea of water, but not a drop comes out. It's terrible! There is a burning sensation, as if some chilli paste has been rubbed on your prick ... as if thorns are being drawn through it ... my eyes pop out with the effort. I have to hold my breath and grind my teeth to let out one drop ... the skin rots and there's only raw flesh ... burning, burning ..."

"Is it syphilis or gonorrhoea?"

"Gonorrhoea. The other causes sores, like blood-red fiery spots ... they cause pain and irritation and grow larger."

"Did you see that male prostitute again?"

"I did and I saw many others like him. Before that I burned that perfumed handkerchief to ashes. He asked me in that raucous, offended, distressed tone why I hadn't gone to him again. Forgotten me? he said. I know why. You are going to someone else, aren't you?"

"All right, now tell me the story of the mother who kicked you on the chest."

MOTHER AND SON

"Exhausted, I sat under a tree, grieving. Behind me rose the ruins of an ancient temple. On my left, at a distance, was the whirring city. Before me stretched a vast solitary wasteland. On my right was an old graveyard. I told you that I was exhausted. I had no money. I flopped down on a slab of stone. Perhaps it was a step leading to some ancient temple. Hunger. Thirst. Exhaustion. Pain. The sun had not set. I dozed off. My cool rocky bed lulled me to sleep. Soon the sun set and night came.

I was unaware of everything. I felt as if someone was calling out to me. Was I in the midst of some commotion? Sweating profusely, I woke up. There was no terrifying darkness. Instead, the world was bathed in moonlight, the moon was peeping through the foliage. Myriad stars dotted the vast sky. The loneliness within me was awakened at the sight of this wide universe. My dormant pain was aroused.

In the din, I could make out the distinctly resentful and pained voice of a woman, Who is that intruder lying there? The voice was directed at me. I didn't move. I didn't utter a word. Though I had never believed in ghosts and spirits, I was really scared. From the distance came another clear voice. An old man's. He said, How does it matter if I am blind in both my eyes?

Glug-glug-glug. Was that a dog lapping up water? And was that the intermittent whimpering of an infant? A female voice, O, haven't I fed my darling? A man's voice, I've got to piss a drop. I didn't hear the piss though.

Din and bustle. People chattering, babies squalling. Where was I? When things became a bit clearer, I was even more frightened. There was a rotten smell – of something being burned. And mingled with it was another smell.

Get up and leave, said the first woman again. She was close to me. I didn't move. Leaves stirred in the gentle wind. I didn't move. The moving shadows fell on my body too. White clouds raced through the sky. They came between the moon and the earth. O heavens, o starry multitudes, o wondrous universe!

Will it rain? a male voice asked from a distance.

God won't let it happen, said a woman in reply.

Why were you lying on the wayside? a man asked someone.

A woman said, I passed out ... Why? ... I gave birth to a baby yesterday ... Who's the father? ... Who knows? ... Stupid woman, someone remarked, followed by guffaws, of men *and* women.

Then the voices came from all directions. An old timer's advice, You should ask a hundred people. That's true, said a woman, Breasts are only for cry-babies ... Glug-glug-glug ... Bow-wow-wow ... Heard that people in this city are god-fearing. Some of them feed five hundred poor people every day, some one hundred, others ten ... But to get the food you have to say that you belong to their religion and caste! ... So you must not tell the truth ... Tell the truth and you get killed ...

Eleven years since I came here ... And what have you earned? a woman's query ... Shit ... Shit? ... Get lost, you slut. Earning, she says! It's she who does all the earning ... But why do you have to stretch your rotten feet towards my face? ... Rotten? It's your fucking cunt that is rotten.

Get up and leave, the woman next to me said again, Isn't this my place? She prodded me with her fingers. I froze like a lump of ice.

Are you dead? she asked me. I didn't move. Let her take me for dead. Sweet smell. Soap? Talcum powder? Probably some cheap perfume. A bit too strong though. I turned my head to the right a little. And then I saw her quite clearly – a woman carrying a little child on her hip. Mother and child!

She stood aside and began to suckle her baby. Large breasts. And the baby sucking away holding the other breast in its soft palm. You know I was never suckled by a mother? O my unknown unseen mother!

My son, my darling child, she was saying, Drink your fill, darling, and go to sleep. Someone is coming to see your amma. He will give us a lot of money. Sleep, my son. She kissed the baby and put it down on a tattered piece of cloth.

In the dark, lonely street, wrapped in rags, orphaned, with the wide sky above. A gentle glowing sun. Tender breeze. The pain of solitude gripped my heart.

The woman tidied her crumpled clothes, covered her bulging breasts and tightened her bodice to make them jut out. Breasts! She loosened and redid her hair, and then stood leaning against the ruined wall of the ancient temple. Waiting.

Who was she waiting for? What expectancy! My heart beat faster. A strange warmth suffused my body.

Nothing to be proud of! A woman's voice rose from the general hubbub. Answering someone, she said, My mother gave birth to me in a gutter. Still I managed to get two husbands and nine children! ... Mother says my father is in the military.

I had a motor car drive today! That was a young woman's voice. Another asked, Who rode you?

Ra-Ri-Ra-Ra-Ro. A lullaby. A woman singing her child to sleep. And then a communal brawl ... What business do they have here? It's broken down, but it's ours ... Get lost, you son of a bitch! It's ours ... Neither yours nor their's. It's ours. We have proof ... Hey, why are you quarrelling about this? Give me a puff of your ganja beedi and then fight ... How does it matter if I have lost my sight? the old man said ... You can't see anything? ... What's there to see in this world? I can hear everything ... There are the moon and the stars! ... Shall I tell you a story? ... A blind man telling a story! ...

There I was. In a wayside shrine with no money, no food, and no one beside me.

Give me one more drag on the beedi ... Is this the story? Here comes the ganja, hold it! ... Ouch, cried a woman, The spark fell on my breast. May a thunderbolt strike your head! ... Strike my head, you slut? ...

Then a lover's complaint, There he comes, dead drunk ... My shweet honey ... Yes? ... A kissh! ... You are reeking of toddy! ... Not toddy – it's frandy ... It's toddy! ... You call frandy toddy, an' I will g-g-kill you!

Someone snaps, You ... My wife's mother gave birth to me! ... Yes, I'm your father! ... Agreed! I'm the son! ... No! ... Daughter? ... No! ... Wife? ... No! ... Father? ... I want no father, no mother. Not even God! Who do you want then? ... Mishter Ganja!

A bit of sad news from another corner. Someone said, A man died on the railway track today. His head was severed. It lay staring at the sky with its mouth open ... The sick, the blind, the beggars ... True! ... In the forest, big trees and small trees. And snakes and tigers, lions, bisons, rabbits, rats and elephants ... In the city, mill owners, ministers, presidents, and generals ... Is our blood the same as theirs? ... Blood is red ... Even of dogs and pigs! ... But dogs and pigs can eat anything.

Another voice from a distance asked, Want to hear something new? I thought he would have a lot of money. So I strangled him at a street corner. But there was only a fake one-rupee coin in his pocket ... And what did you do with it? a woman asked.

O, my son, there he comes! said the woman who stood beside me. Who was it? Someone was approaching her. He was now with the woman. A silent, starry sky bathed in moonlight. And below, a crowd. Primordial desires. They were speaking in hushed tones. Then she stopped him, No. Wait. Give me the money first. And then you can start pawing my breasts ... You think only of money. And I come all the way here because I love you ... She laughed, choking with pain, Love and lust can't fill my son's stomach or mine ... How much? ... One rupee. Give it first ... Here it is. One rupee. Woman, have you any disease? ... Disease indeed! ... Haven't you eaten anything today? ... To hell with your fine talk. Do what you want to do and get lost! Enough if I take off my dhoti and stand against this wall?

I wasn't shocked. Nor did I tremble. We poor, weak creatures. Our desires. Everything has to be satisfied, isn't that so? The man must have seen me then. He asked, Who's that? Your ...? ... No! None of mine. Just an intruder. Came and lay down there just like that. Looks as if he is dead! ... Dead? Is it a corpse then?

A little pebble fell on my body. I didn't move ... Corpse all over ... Looks like it. Come on, finish with it and go ... Let's go in there ... Don't you have a house? ... Oh no! You can't come there. My parents and my wife ... So you have a wife? ... She is pregnant ... How many months gone? ... Five-six. Leave the child there and come ... I won't leave my child anywhere!

And my unknown mother abandoning me on the road!

Come sweetheart, I will give you half a rupee more , he said ... You are hurting me. Never seen breasts before, have you? ... Come dear ... And my darling child? ... Just leave it there ... With the corpse? ... The corpse won't eat up the baby, will it? ... That's true ... She covered the baby tenderly with a rag, little realizing there were ants around. Amma will be back soon, she said to it. And she left. The two of them went into the old ruined temple.

The baby and I alone, and the great universe."

THE CITIZEN OF THE FUTURE

"The child was all alone. I got up. Once, I too had been like him. Strange! In the open ground before me, all around me, flames leaped up from little improvised hearths. Hundreds of hearths. Rubbish, waste paper, dry leaves and old rags being used as fuel. Smoke and a foul smell.

General pandemonium. Men, women and little children. And dogs. Faces reflecting the glow of fire. Nothing was distinct. Bloodshot eyes, sweaty faces, beards and moustaches. Beggars' sacks. Women with bosoms uncovered. Many communities. Different kinds of clothes. And only commotion. Eating. Talking. Smoking. Praying. Laughing and weeping. Abusing, embracing, copulating.

Listen, everybody! I am setting off some crackers! says a voice. A flash. Sparks flew, hissing. And the explosion. Tat-tat-tat. It lit up the faces and the bodies of the men and women huddled together. The

lumpens with nothing special to do. Nowhere to go. No name nor land of their own. Nothing. Yet they had everything that human beings need on earth. The citizens of the world are born in that society – without any privacy. They grow up, they procreate. Out in the open.

I went up to the abandoned child. There he was, a future citizen of the world! What did he know of things? Born like you and I and everyone else. He would grow up with passions and desires, grow up to be a man with a moustache and a beard. And scattering semen all around, he will procreate too, then become grey with age and die. Or he may die a premature death. Were he to grow up, which faith would he follow? Whatever his mother has told him would remain indelibly imprinted on his little heart. And growing up, he would decide that his belief was superior to the beliefs of others. But now, there he was – not a Hindu, a Christian, Muslim, Jew, Parsi, Buddhist nor Sikh, but a little child born of man and woman.

You and I are children born of men and women. Now I have turned out this way. What is the future of that child? Will he have the same experiences as I have had? Will he become stricken with diseases? Perhaps he will turn out a beggar, a thief or a poet, or perhaps a politician, a scientist or the prophet of a new religion.

All of a sudden, there was a loud rumbling sound. Br-rr-rr-rum-boom-br-rr-rr-rim! An aeroplane! A hundred voices shouted, Plane, plane. Aeroplanes remind one of the war.

Two green stars approached. A red one too. And they swept past us with a terrible roar, as if tearing through everything. Silence. Again the uproar of voices, as if a giant machine had been restarted.

Suddenly, the abandoned child beside me began to yell. When its cries became unbearable, I picked it up. It had been bitten by hundreds of ants. I put the child on my lap and started picking out the ants from his body.

O my child, the agonized mother came running, hearing her child's screams. She snatched the child from me and gave me a violent kick on my chest! I didn't say a word. I sat down where I had been lying.

My head was spinning. The woman began to feed the child. She must have realized what had happened when the ants bit into her breasts.

A voice rose from the din, Keep quiet! ...

What if I don't have eyes? I can remember, can't I? ... Remember what? ... Once upon a time, I was sitting at a wayside shrine, with no money, no food, and no one beside me. That day our country got independence from the white sahebs! I was twenty then ...

Oh, my darling little baby, did those ants bite you and try to kill you? ... The child stopped crying and sucked at his mother's breasts.

The blind man's voice came from a distance, That day I asked myself, Why should you live? And I had no answer. How old am I today? Think about it. Last night, when all of you had gone to sleep, I sat up and asked myself ...

Beggar man, the poor mother came up to me with the child, I thought you were dead! Did it hurt when I kicked you?

I didn't say anything. My eyes welled up with tears

You picked up the child when the ants bit him? ... Yes ... I thought you were going to steal him!

She took out a quarter-rupee coin from a knot in her dhoti and dropped it on my lap. You can lie down there if you want! she said.

She moved away and lay down on a step. I asked no questions. I said nothing. A mother's heart with love for her little one.

Voices. I ... I kept hearing voices. My eyes brimmed over with tears. I felt as if my heart had broken into a thousand fragments. I lay there. O world, I lay there!

Something rumbled inside my head. I opened my eyes. Bright sunlight. Silence. No one around. The old temple in ruins. That was all. The quarter-rupee coin lay beside me. I sat up. The whole maidan was empty. Pockmarked with hearth stones. Like charred sores. The whirring of the city could be heard from a distance.

I picked up the coin. It was hot to touch. I walked towards the city, holding it."

AT INFINITY'S EDGE

"I had been walking aimlessly along crowded streets. Electric lights shone far brighter than the stars. The city was teeming with its countless denizens. Vast and expansive as the sky. Yet I was all alone.

I entered a street that exuded a certain fragrance. In the houses that faced the street were women, all dressed up, glossy hair decked with jasmine flowers. Their faces were powdered, their lips painted red. Gleaming eyes blackened with kajal. The women wore thin, transparent clothes that revealed their contours. There was a heady fragrance of jasmine, champak, roses – an onrush of expectancy dense with the fragrance of flowers and the scent of unguents. Hands, buttocks, thighs, breasts and lips beckoned you. O the great universe!

What a commotion there was in the street! People laughing, singing, making merry. Pay and choose your woman. A market for female flesh. Joints where you could gratify your lust. People from all walks of life were there. Some people went in openly, nonchalantly. Others went on the sly, casting furtive glances all around. I was overcome by a sense of utter loneliness. I walked on aimlessly and reached the seashore.

Lots of men and women walked on the wide white beach, their cars parked on the roadside. They had come to take in some fresh air. Listening to them I could make out what professions they belonged to. They were all passing time, engaged in animated arguments and hearty conversation. Soon they would all return home.

Leaving them behind, I walked on the beach. Silence all around. I saw a number of battered boats, probably fishermen's boats. I got into one of them and sat down. The white foamy sea raged before me. It was as if a hot vapour was rising. But everything else was still. Exhausted, I lay down, and thought about my sad fate.

Not a soul in this world either to love me or hate me. There were countless human beings on this earth – and what a variety! Was there any difference between me and the rest of them? Yet there was no bond between us, not one meant anything to me. Or, as you said earlier, all of them were related to me, they were my own kith and kin. But this thought didn't give me even the slightest consolation.

You can say anything you like in poetry. It is all rhetoric. But in real life the brutal truth is that each one of us is an isolated creature. What does it matter if someone dies or someone lives? Maybe all of us are part of a community. If this is true, bacteria, worms, reptiles, birds, animals and trees – all are distant relatives of the human community.

Haven't I told you – my life and thoughts have always been disorganized, lacking order and coherence? I am merely a lonely being, not even a cog in the giant machine called humankind. To be honest, no one has ever shown any kindness to me. Even if someone had ... I wonder if I had enough affection for my foster father while he lived. Now that he is no more, I love his memory.

On the whole my heart was filled with sorrow. I thought of taking my life on the railway track. Weeping bitterly, I fell asleep.

Boundless silence. A bitter cold. I opened my eyes. Darkness. Not pitch dark, but a strange blend of light and darkness, like the primeval night before the dawn of history. This was what occurred to me at that time. The stars were dim. Where was I? Suddenly I remembered ...

I wondered how long it would take for the sun to rise. I could not gauge anything clearly. My clothes were wet. I got out of the boat and stepped on the sand. The soles of my feet were numb with cold. The top layer of the sand was quite wet. I swept it aside with my foot. Beneath, it was still dry and warm. I sat down.

The sea was a vast dense stretch of darkness. A terrifying loneliness touched the very core of my heart, through every pore of my body. All of a sudden I remembered the cold, primeval sense of things. God is the last refuge of the lonely and the destitute. For a while I was immersed in that thought. Tears welled up in my eyes, I didn't know why or what for. It would not be right to say that I thought of all the people in this world. How could I think of those whom I had never met? After all, my heart was not large enough to contain the whole universe.

It would be truer to say that I just sat there, without a thought in my head. And then a certain sense of vitality began to stir within me. I attribute this to the change of colour in the horizon, auguring the birth of a new day. How many, many new days have swept past us! And now yet another new day ... Indeterminate sounds and voices in the world ... What kind of day would this be? But however much I thought, I had no clue whatsoever about it.

Sounds and voices. Sirens from mills and factories summoning the workers – the workers of the world. Loud, hollow whistles from ships. There was no one to call me. No man nor machine. One more day was about to dawn. A glowing golden orb rising from the brink of the deep ink-blue stretch of sea. The sun.

For a moment it was a wondrous sea of blood. Then it turned into a stretch of molten gold. And then it began to shine like a sheet of glass. I rose to my feet.

My shadow lengthened and stretched out beyond the city. To the boundless edges of the infinite! Go, go!"

THE CLANG OF THE RAIL TRACKS

"And then?"

"The clanging railway tracks resounded in my ears! That's what I have to talk to you about now. Feeling sleepy?"

"No, I am listening and taking down everything."

"I don't have much more to say. We're coming to the last part. What's your opinion about all that I've already said?"

"My opinion? I have recorded everything. Now I have to compile it. But I'll have to go somewhere else to do that."

"Go where?"

"Some place where I can be all alone and write in peace. You can stay here till I come back. I'll give you some money and introduce you to a doctor friend of mine. He will give you medicines. I'll come back and read out your story, all right? Now tell me the rest of it."

"What do you think of suicide?"

"Is it right or wrong?"

"Yes."

"I have never felt like committing suicide. Let's assume that life at its best is a failure, considering the fact that one has to die if one is born. But one must live courageously till one dies, with the full awareness of being a human being who is part of this great universe ... This has been my view so far."

"Live to do what?"

"Anything. The whole world is before you. There will be something or the other that you can do. Chalk out a plan of action ... Suppose you want to become the president of this country, try to attain that position. You don't have to worry about success or failure. Make an attempt, that's all. I wish you success."

"Didn't I tell you that I do not have a philosophy of life? What plan of action can I draw out? The house that is me is in ruins. I've no mother. No father. No one. I am all alone in this world. Didn't I tell you, there is not a soul to love me or even hate me? That's why I asked you about suicide."

"Haven't you ever felt happy? Never experienced well-being?"

"Only in a dream."

"What do you mean?"

"Eating when I am hungry, quenching my thirst, warming myself by a fire when I feel cold, sleeping when I'm tired – yes, I've felt happy doing such things."

"And then?"

"The sunrise, the rising moon, fragrant flowers, beautiful women, music – all these have given me joy."

"And?"

"Getting drunk, getting high on drugs – yes, that too."

"What else?"

"Scratching myself where it itches, pissing when I feel like it. If you look at it that way, life is full of happiness, isn't it?"

"Have you ever done anything all by yourself and felt the pleasure of doing it? Farming, for instance ... planting at least one seedling and watching it grow, bloom and bring forth fruit. Or making something new, or giving water to a thirsty dog, or giving food to a hungry man? Things like that."

"You know that all I have done by myself is shoot and kill people. And I have drunk the blood of men. Once I even tried to kill myself."

"And what happened?"

"Let me tell you about that as well, and I will leave this very night."

"Where will you go?"

"Why, isn't this my birthplace? Let me try to trace my parents. I will walk into every house, asking every woman if she is my mother, the woman who gave birth to me and then left me wrapped up in rags at the crossroads in the middle of the night. Even after my death I'll haunt every house. I'll knock at each door till my eyes pop out."

"Please stop! You can do all this after I write your story and read it out to you. Now tell me about your suicide attempt. How did it go wrong?"

"Yes, I decided to kill myself. I wanted to be crushed to death by a speeding train ... With my neck on the railway track. I would lie down, the wheels would grind me to pulp and move on. My head with gaping eyes would be severed from the body. Everything would be over, it would be an end to all my pain and misery.

A quiet, moonlit night. I sat beneath a tree near the unfrequented railway tracks in a corner of the city. Haven't you noticed how the tracks reverberate, ringing in your ears? Every half an hour there was a train.

A train sped past roaring. I crossed the barbed fence and lay down on one of the tracks. Lay down for the last time in my life. A chill passed through my neck. The next day, I would be an unidentified, unclaimed corpse. Unclaimed in the real sense of the term. It was time for another train to come. I heard a whirring, rumbling sound ... Brr-rr-rum br-rr-rr-rum! An aeroplane. At the same time a train came along too. The tracks were clanging in my ears. I was scared and confused. It is a feeling you can understand only if you have lain with your neck on the track. Two or three times I felt like springing to my feet and running away. But I didn't move. My eardrums were about to burst.

Then there was a whistle that sent shock waves through the earth and the sky! It must have been heard all over the universe! The train was racing towards me. Racing. I shut my eyes. Stopped breathing. Broke out into a sweat. There was a burning inside my head. God, I lay waiting for the final moment when my neck would be crushed. And the train with its deafening clangour sped past me screeching and wailing, along the track next to where I lay."

"And then?"

"That's it. Mangalam!"

This story was first published as "Sabdangal" in 1947.

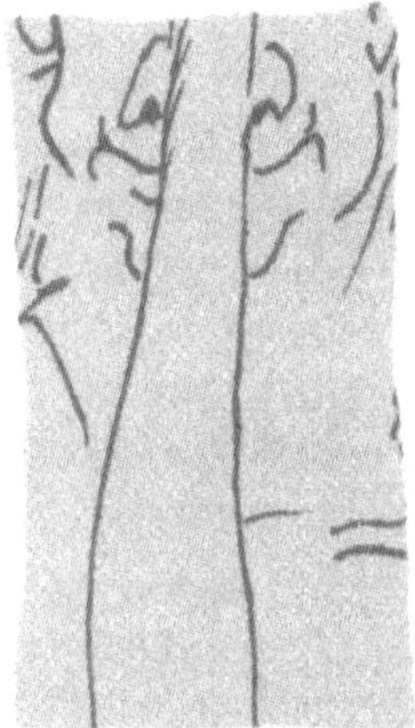

The world-renowned nose

Stunning news – a nose is the subject of heated debates and arguments among intellectuals! I record here the true history of that nose.

The story begins at the point where our hero entered the twenty-fourth year of his life. I wonder whether there is anything special about that age. If you care to look into the annals of history, I am sure you will find something remarkable about the twenty-fourth year in the lives of all great men. It is needless, of course, to point this fact out to students of history.

Our hero was a poor illiterate cook, not particularly known for his intelligence. His kitchen was his world. He was not bothered by anything that happened outside it. And why should he be? His routine consisted of cooking, eating heartily, taking a good pinch of snuff, sleeping, waking up and busying himself with his cooking again.

Mookken did not even know the names of the days or the months. His mother would come to collect his wages when they were due. She would bring him his snuff. Thus, he lived happy and contented till the twenty-fourth year of his life.

And then – it happened!

Mookken's nose started growing all of a sudden – it extended past his mouth and down his chin in no time. Within a month, its tip was level with his navel. It was not something you could hide from people's gaze for long. But did it make Mookken uncomfortable in any way? Not

translated by
K M Sherrif

a bit. The nose still did what all noses usually do – breathe, take in snuff, distinguish one smell from another. It behaved like a perfectly normal nose.

Perhaps there was nothing unusual about it. The occurrence of such noses have been recorded in history. But do you think *this* was just another of those rare cases of nasal aberrations? No, it definitely was not. For, this nose got our poor hero dismissed from his job.

No union fought for his reinstatement. All political parties turned a blind eye to this act of gross injustice. No philanthropist cared to raise this issue. Where were our socially conscious intellectuals and philosophers when Mookken, a poor cook, was thrown out into the street? But then, he was a mere kitchen hand.

Mookken knew very well why he was being dismissed. The family that employed him had not had a moment's peace after his nose started growing. Large crowds gathered before the house to take a look at his nose. Photographers, reporters, TV crews ... it was a roaring sea of humanity that laid siege on the house. It was burgled several times and there was even an attempt to kidnap the attractive, teenaged daughter of the family.

As he languished in his humble hut, the poor retrenched cook was forced to concede that his nose had acquired everlasting fame. People continued to arrive from far and near to have a look at it. Amazed by the sight, some of them even ventured to touch it.

But nobody, not a soul, bothered to ask him why he looked so weak or whether he had had any lunch. There was not a paisa at home to buy even a pinch of snuff. Was he a starving animal on exhibition? At last, he called his mother and whispered to her, "Tell those horrid pests to leave me alone and shut the door on their faces." Mookken's mother tactfully persuaded the curious visitors to disperse and closed the front door.

This proved to be a turning point in Mookken's life. Fortune smiled

---

Mookken: A name not uncommon in Kerala, it means one who has an extraordinarily long or big nose.

on the old mother and her young illustrious son. Thousands of visitors, their curiosity not satisfied, offered to pay to take a look at Mookken's nose. After all, the mob is a stupid lot, isn't it?

A group of conscientious intellectuals did raise their voice against what they described as "an open swindle." But their protests fell on deaf ears. The government initiated no action against Mookken. Enraged at this criminal abdication of responsibility on the part of the government, the conscientious intellectuals joined hands with subversives and saboteurs of various shades.

Mookken's income increased. To cut a long story short, in six years' time, our poor illiterate cook became a well-known millionaire. He acted in three films. *The Human Submarine*, the technicolour extravaganza on his life attracted millions of viewers. Six renowned poets wrote encomiums on Mookken. Nine biographies were published, earning fame and money for Mookken's biographers. He kept open house at his mansion. Anybody could get a free meal for the asking. A pinch of snuff too!

Mookken had two secretaries. Both were charming and educated. Both loved Mookken ardently. It may be mentioned here that there are some women who can always be relied upon to fall in love with even highway robbers or homicidal maniacs. If you turn the pages of history, you will find that there has always been trouble when two women have loved the same man. This happened in Mookken's life too.

Like his beautiful secretaries, the general public too loved Mookken to distraction. If a universally acclaimed nose, long and beautiful, reaching down to the navel, is not a sign of greatness, then what is?

Mookken gave statements on all events of international importance. The reporters jotted his words down eagerly. "Talking to newsmen about the introduction of the new generation of jets capable of flying at speeds up to 10,000 miles per hour, Mr Mookken remarked that ..." or "After Dr Bundros Furasiburos announced his miraculous success

in bringing a dead patient back to life, Mr Mookken commented ..."
When news came about the conquest of the highest peak in the world,
people asked one another: Well, what does Mookken think about it?
If he did not have anything to say about it ... tcha, the matter was of no
consequence at all!

Soon Mookken's views were solicited on a variety of subjects – the
origin of the universe, interplanetary travel, photography, the painter's
art, techniques in fiction, the publishing industry, journalism, killing
animals for sport, mesmerism, the existence of the soul and life after
death ... There was nothing under the sun or beyond it that Mookken
was not aware of.

At this juncture, a series of conspiracies were initiated and plots
hatched to appropriate Mookken. If you have read enough of history,
you will know there is nothing very original about appropriation. In
fact, the history of human society is the history of appropriations.
What do I mean by appropriation? Let me illustrate. You plant a few
coconut saplings on a plot of uncultivated land. Fence it. Water the
plants everyday. Years pass. The saplings grow into tall handsome
trees, heavy with bunches of large coconuts. Anybody who sees the
grove is tempted and tries to grab it by hook or by crook. This is
appropriation.

The first attempt was made by the government. It was indeed a
clever ploy! The government conferred on Mookken the title of "Chief
of the Long-nosed Worthies" and awarded him a gold medal. The
medal was given away by the President at a special ceremony. Instead
of shaking Mookken's hand, the President shook his long nose. The
newsreels of the function were shown on television and in cinema
halls across the length and breadth of the country.

It was the turn of the political parties next. Comrade Mookken
should lead the historical struggle of the people! "Comrade" Mookken?

Poor Mookken! He was unwittingly dragged into politics. But which
party should he join? There were many. The prime objective of all of
them was to bring about a people's revolution. But Mookken could

not possibly give his allegiance to all the people's revolutionary parties at the same time.

Mookken said to himself, "Why should I join any party? Oh, I can't be bothered with all this!"

One of his secretaries seized the opportunity. "Comrade Mookken, you must join my party if you really love me."

Mookken said nothing.

"Should I join any of these parties?" he asked the other damsel.

She immediately understood what was going on in his mind. "Oh, why should you?" she said with a shrug of her shoulders.

But the workers of one revolutionary party were convinced that Mookken was their man. "Comrade Mookken zindabad! People's Revolutionary Party zindabad!" the slogans resounded.

The other people's revolutionary parties were not pleased with this development. They forced one of his secretaries to give a damaging statement to the press.

> I regret the fact that Mookken, the worst bourgeois reactionary of our times, made me a party to the appalling fraud he devised. I apologize to the people. Let me reveal, though belatedly, the truth about Mookken's nose. It is only a piece of rubber!

All the newspapers in the world splashed the news on their front pages: Long-nosed miracle exposed! A clever conman! A political opportunist preying on the gullible public! The connivance of the powers that be – natural nose, what nonsense!

It was only logical that the news should send shock waves through the centres of power. The President was bombarded with telegrams, phone calls and letters. "Death to the Chief of the Rubber-nosed Worthies! Down with Mookken's reactionary clique! Inquilab zindabad!" shouted the workers of the People's Revolutionary Party (Anti-Mookken).

But the People's Revolutionary Party (Pro-Mookken) soon joined the fray. The result was a press statement by Mookken's other secretary!

Comrades and friends! My colleague has distinguished herself with convincing but totally fabricated lies. Her statement is merely a piece of malicious propaganda. She is taking revenge on Mookken for having spurned her advances. As everybody knows, she only wanted Comrade Mookken's money and the mileage she got from being his secretary. Besides, her brother is a member of that party of shameless opportunists who *call* themselves People's Revolutionary Party. I use this opportunity to expose them for the scoundrels and bloodsuckers they are. As the trusted and loyal secretary of Comrade Mookken, I know his nose is natural – and as true as my heart. I salute the people who have rallied behind the leadership of Comrade Mookken in this hour of crisis. Comrade Mookken zindabad! People's Revolutionary Party zindabad! Inquilab zindabad!

What were the people to make of all this? There was utter confusion everywhere. The People's Revolutionary Party (Anti-Mookken) hurled a volley of accusations against the government. "It is obvious to all, except the most gullible, why Mookken was made the Chief of the Long-nosed Worthies and awarded a gold medal studded with diamonds. The President and the Prime Minister are directly involved in this gross deception of the people. No doubt, it is part of a wider conspiracy. The President has to go – and the Prime Minister too. The best thing under the circumstances is for the whole cabinet to resign. The rubber-nosed swindler must be brought to book at the earliest."

The President was provoked. So was the Prime Minister. Tanks rolled towards Mookken's mansion. He was arrested.

There was no news of Mookken for several days after that. People forgot Mookken and his nose. Everything was calm and peaceful.

And then the President dropped a bombshell! When Mookken had almost faded from everybody's memory, there was this communique from the President's office.

> There will be a public trial on the ninth day of March of
> Mr Mookken, Chief of the Long-nosed Worthies, who is
> now under detention facing charges of fabricating a
> rubber nose of extraordinary dimensions and extorting
> money from the people by exhibiting it as a natural nose.
> Medical experts from forty-eight countries will examine
> this nose in order to determine whether it is natural or
> artificial. Reporters representing all the major dailies of
> the world and radio and TV crews will be present on the
> occasion. People are requested to remain calm.

But the people were an asinine lot. They did not remain calm.
They flocked to the capital, raided restaurants, ransacked newspaper
offices, burnt down movie theatres, looted liquor shops and destroyed
police stations and government installations. There were several
communal clashes. Hundreds of men and women became martyrs in
the cause of Mookken's nose.

March 9: Millions of people congregated on the lawns and roads
near the Presidential Palace. When the clock struck eleven, the
loudspeakers positioned around the palace boomed, "People are
requested to maintain self-restraint."

The medical experts surrounded the Chief of the Long-nosed
Worthies in the presence of the President and the Prime Minister.
The multitude, which had gathered outside, waited with bated breath.

One of the medical experts blocked Mookken's nose. Mookken
opened his mouth. Another expert pricked the tip of Mookken's long
nose with a pin. And ... wonder of wonders! A drop of blood appeared
on the tip of the celebrated controversial nose.

"The nose is flesh and blood. It is natural." The verdict of the
medical experts was unanimous.

Mookken's trusted and loyal secretary, who had stood by him
through thick and thin, kissed him passionately on the tip of his long
venerable nose.

"Comrade Mookken zindabad! People's Revolutionary Party zindabad! Hands off Comrade Mookken's respected nose!" The slogans shook the walls of the Presidential Palace.

When the slogans died down, the President came up with another of his shrewd manoeuvres. It was announced over the loudspeakers that Mr Mookken would soon be honoured with a Mookkashri and nominated to the Parliament.

Mookkashri Mookken, MP!

A prestigious university honoured Mookken with an MLitt, while another went a step further and conferred a DLitt on him.

Mookkashri Mookken, Master of Literature!

Mookkashri Mookken, Doctor of Literature!

But the People's Revolutionary Party (Anti-Mookken) formed a united front to fight the government. Undeterred by the verdict of the medical experts, they cried,

Down with the President!

Down with the Prime Minister!

Death to Mookken and his rubber nose!

Death to the abetters of this colossal fraud on the people!

As they say, the course of people's revolution never did run smooth! And the conscientious intellectuals? What were they to make of all the din and confusion? Oh, the poor intellectuals!

This story was first published as "Viswavikhyatamaya Mookku" in the anthology of the same name (1954).

A devil

What is that noise? The dogs must have seen something to moan like this. Even at midnight, when it is pitch dark, they seem to see strange presences. And then run around, sniffing.

The devil? Do I know for sure whether it exists or not? Well, listen to me – the devil, the bhoot, the anamarutai, the chattan, in short, every single shaitan exists.

The anamarutai? It haunts the world at midnight with its blazing eyes and goes about dragging its fetters and trumpeting. Maybe it exists. I don't know. But I do know of a person who had seen a host of skeletons playing with fireballs on a Friday.

One midnight, standing in the middle of a field, he saw a strange fiery glow rise and touch the sky. The very next moment he heard a thunderous roar and the fire died out. Again it rose, followed by heart-chilling laughter. The scattered blazes looked like blood-smeared, headless trunks dancing around as if at a devils' carnival. He was a brave soul. But he fell unconscious as soon as he reached home. For three months, he suffered from loss of memory and talked incoherently.

The man I am talking about was known to be a social worker. They say he had a number of enemies, all of whom he destroyed. You ask me how? In a most sinister manner. He would bribe a tea-stall keeper to mix a certain acid in the tea he served to his enemies. This went on for six

translated by
Vanajam Ravindran

months. The victims did not die physically, but their spirit was so crushed that they were never the same men again. Subsequently, the social worker took his own life by slashing his jugular vein.

Such weird things keep happening all the time right before our eyes. Destroying your enemies by poisoning their food with acid is nothing new. If we are courageous enough to embark on soul-searching voyages, we will all discover the devils in our own selves.

Put out that lamp, don't you know kerosene is very expensive now? This is wartime. And make sure you don't knock down the lamp with your hand. Darkness is, in fact, a source of comfort. In the silence of darkness all faded memories assume clarity.

What is that scratching sound from above? Must be a frightened cat on the roof looking down at the scared dogs running helter-skelter. Here, toss the match-box to me. You must be wondering about the thin match sticks. In an economy drive I split each stick into four. A match can be split even into six or eight parts if you have the skill. I need to keep a match-box or torch under my pillow. It has become a habit ever since I had a hair-raising experience at Tumkur in 1933. The mere thought of it makes my heart pound. This is not fantasy nor fiction but something that really happened. My beloved says that a story shouldn't deal with a real experience.

Incidentally, I have become slave to a consuming passion, an unquenchable thirst. Are you laughing at me? Yes, desire too is a devil, in a sense. A demon that tosses you from the depths of hell to the heights of paradise. She is nameless. I used to call her "my dear Helen of Troy." Incredible, the number of passionate letters I wrote to her. Yes, she did respond. But imagine my dismay when she said that it was filial love ... How dare you say that my Helen is a devil! You are bored stiff, I know. All right, go to sleep. Good night!

Tumkur? It is in the state of Mysore. For nine or ten years, I was constantly on the move. There was no place I didn't visit, no job I didn't try my hand at and no disguise I did not assume. My intention was to go to Russia via Afghanistan, but since I was travelling at a snail's pace, it took me five long years to reach the Khyber Pass from Vaikom. So, feeling a little diffident, I decided to return ...

That creaky sound? Must be some dog prowling around and sniffing at dry leaves.

My experience at Tumkur? I don't think it is wise to narrate such a story on an eerie night like this. It is about a devil. You will be scared, let me warn you.

All right, but don't keep interrupting me with questions. Just listen.

We were great travellers those days – my friend and I. He was from Paravoor. Sivaraman Kartav. Of more or less my age. Tall, thin, brown of complexion, with bright eyes, a shapely nose and thin lips. He always had a winsome smile beaming on his rather flat face. But his teeth were never exposed. There was something nice about his gruff voice. He was incapable of displeasing anybody. He was the only person I didn't quarrel with in the course of my travels.

At least ten times a day, Kartav would remind me that he was my greatest asset. He took care of all the practical aspects of our many engagements. Although he looked upon me as a callow youth, he was rather scared of me and, consulted me in all matters. The understanding between us was that I would handle the cash. This was because he was a compulsive buyer! Though he was not inordinately fond of food, he nevertheless had an urge to buy all kinds of eatables. He would buy them on the pretext that they were for me. As if I was hankering after them!

Our customary way of addressing each other was "Eh, Pillai!" When the school-term was on, we would go about making public speeches. He would learn, by rote, the speeches I wrote out and then deliver them with great aplomb in impeccable English. A great story teller, he once held forth on how I had waged an hour-long fight with a tiger and how, finally, I had swung it around, holding it by its tail, and dashed its head against a boulder. And how I, sporting a hunter's outfit, had looked down bashfully, the cynosure of hundreds of beautiful eyes. The listeners had been all praise for Kartav's eloquence. "What style! And he is not even a graduate!"

Anyway, our stint in Tumkur was during the school-break. It is a small city surrounded by a wasteland dotted with hillocks and ponds. Water was scarce there, and the ponds were utilized mainly for irrigation. In the afternoons, the view from a hillock was quite interesting – the little ponds looked like numerous shining bits of mica. The streams had been reduced to beds of white sand due to the hot summer. Only in Mysore does one come across well-water of so many different tastes – brackish, lime-like, sour, bitter, sulphurous.

We were staying in a guest house on the banks of a stream. One afternoon, I was woken from my nap by a knock on the door and accompanied by Kartav's peremptory order, "Pillai, open the door."

Opening the door, my eyes fell on a stranger. A short, dark man, with cropped hair, a button-nose, and close-set light eyes. He was wearing a khadi kurta and dhoti, and carried a thick cane. He must have been in his early thirties. Kartav introduced him. "This is Pandit Narasimhan. He is a teacher in the girls' school and a reputed scholar of Hindi. He wanted to meet you."

As I had a smattering of Hindi, we soon became friends. I was impressed by Pandit Narasimhan's sensible conversation. His light eyes remained clear and still when he laughed. On the whole, his was an attractive personality. We chatted for half an hour.

After Narasimhanji left, Kartav complimented me on my urbane behaviour. I lost my temper and retorted, "As if I am otherwise a boor! You think that you are the only one endowed with social graces!"

Kartav burst out laughing. Then, attempting to mollify me, he said, "Look Pillai, I didn't mean that. He is someone who matters – a social worker with a lot of political clout. Now that school is closed, he conducts Hindi classes and gives private tuitions to the daughters of government officials. If he is inclined to favour us, we should be able to make a substantial collection from here."

In the course of those five days of close association with Narasimhanji, I was convinced of Kartav's estimate of his importance. Pandit Narasimhan was not merely influential, he was held in high esteem by the people, the rich as well as the poor. The government officials as well. Our cash collection from Tumkur was much more than we had expected.

We had intended to leave Tumkur at the crack of dawn. Kartav, who was packing up, insisted that I should go and formally take leave of Pandit Narasimhan. He sent a Kannadiga boy, a student of the Hindi teacher, to accompany me. He lived within the school premises in a suburb of the town. The school was in the middle of a playground.

As the student and I walked on, our conversation turned to the subject of ghosts. I narrated one from my ample repertoire of ghost stories. A tale about a black bhoot, as tall as a mountain, seated on my chest and smothering me. My companion then told me of an experience of his. Once, when he was alone in the woods, four people had accosted him. One of them was killed and his skin flayed by the other three who not only indulged in cannibalistic feasting but compelled my companion to eat human flesh too. But that was more a nightmare than a real ghost story, I thought. He then narrated another experience of his. It was about the ghost of a woman carrying around her dead child. He claimed that others had seen her too.

By then it was after ten and we were far from the town. It was pitch dark and a dry wind whistled. In the light of the stars, the black silhouette of the school building assumed a baneful aspect. The oppressive silence was now and again broken by the murmuring wind.

Reaching the house, we saw a thin streak of light through a chink in the window. Knocking on the window, I called out, "Narasimhanji!"

Bhoot: Because of his extensive travelling, Basheer's Malayalam contains a number of Hindi and Urdu words like bhoot, shaitan etc.

So did my companion, in Kannada. There was no response. We continued to knock on the door. In vain. I suggested that Narasimhanji must have gone to bed.

"He never goes to bed this early," said my companion. "Let's try the other door."

Crossing the playground, we went through a little garden to the front side. The reflection of neon lights from the public road fell on the dark steps. His room was at the northern corner of the hall. We entered the hall. The howling of foxes reached us through the whistling wind. My companion followed me as I groped in the dark, trying to avoid the numerous columns in the hall. We could easily have knocked our heads against them. There were so many of them there.

As I gingerly moved, step by step, my hand came in contact with something soft and cold. I heard a stifled moan. Suddenly that thing clutched at me. I stood stunned for a moment, covered with gooseflesh. Though I was not frightened, I could not utter a word.

As I tried to free myself from its clutches, my hand touched a soft naked body – an ample bosom, dishevelled hair. I could make out that it was holding something between its teeth. No more details could be gathered in the dark. I broke out in a cold sweat. My heart pounded. I felt countless beetles buzz inside my head. That creature was breathing. Its heart was beating.

As I stood nonplussed, my companion anxiously asked, "What is it?"

Breathlessly, I whispered, "A woman!"

"A woman?"

"Yes. Light a match stick."

"But I don't have a match-box," he said apologetically.

"Doesn't matter. Turn around and walk on quietly."

After disentangling myself from the hands that clutched my waist, I gripped its hand and turned back. There was something creeping behind us. I wondered what it was.

Panting and groping in the dark, we found ourselves at the door. My heart literally froze.

It was a naked girl. Dark. Nubile. Gagged with a red saree.

We removed the gag and she started breathing normally. Promptly she covered herself with the saree. As she did so, a four-anna coin dropped on the door step with a clink. Shamefaced, she picked it up. Then sobbing, she answered my companion's queries in Kannada. Now and again, she turned to look at me with large frightened eyes. I could not understand anything. But my companion's face was completely drained of blood. Removing his cap, he started to fan himself. She pointed to a little hut across the road, and raising her tear-drenched face towards me, said, "Ayyah, I ..."

Tears coursed down her face, which was flushed with fear and panic. She descended the steps and walked on, wiping her downcast face with the end of her saree. When she finally reached the hut, she turned in our direction once, and then the door shut, its creaking sound merged with the murmuring wind.

Sighing deeply, my companion told me, "She is the daughter of the woman who supplies milk to the Hindi master. Toda ..." His grief-stricken expression pierced my heart.

I made no comments. As my eyes fell on a few drops of blood on the doorstep, my companion turned his face away. Overwhelmed by acute embarrassment, he asked me, "Do you want to see Panditji?"

"Hm. Not necessary." I said noncommittally.

Yet I turned towards the hall and called out loudly, "Narasimhanji, we are leaving early tomorrow morning. I came to bid my final farewell."

The hall resounded with my voice. And again assumed its silence. The streak of light that we had seen through the chink in the window had disappeared.

"You are really brave," remarked my companion.

I said nothing.

We walked back in silence. He took leave of me at his doorstep. It was a farewell fraught with despair, disillusion and disgust. Among the many farewells I have bidden, this one stands out in my memory.

As if in a trance, I walked up to the guest house.

"Hey, Pillai, how was your meeting with Panditji? I hope you didn't have an argument with him," asked Kartav in his characteristic bluff manner.

I couldn't respond. I felt I was smeared with foulness.

Astonished at my state, Kartav stared at me from head to foot and got up. Then suddenly, pointing to my dhoti, he asked, "What are those blood stains?"

"Blood?"

Yes, it was blood from the yoni. My entire soul was shaken as I looked at the three or four red spots on my white dhoti. Filled with revulsion, I took it off and cast it aside. Then lighting a match stick, I set fire to the discarded garment, against the backdrop of the moaning wind and the howling foxes.

Kartav's face glowed in the light of the rising flame. I watched the dhoti being reduced to charred bits – the first khadi apparel that I cremated.

Panic-stricken, Kartav looked into my eyes and, holding me by my shoulders, shook me vigorously. "Come on Pillai, what's all this? What has come over you? What's the meaning of this? "

"Meaning?" I muttered.

All that remained of the dhoti was some black ash. With my foot I pushed it into the courtyard. From there it was blown off by the wind.

Back in our room I lit a beedi. Kartav paced to and fro, observing me through the corner of his eye. Realizing that he was concerned about my state, I narrated the entire experience to him.

His face cleared up. "Look, you had better have a bath before going to bed. I am really amazed. You didn't get scared? You managed to drag the creature into the light?"

That chilly night I was forced to have a bath in brackish water. Early next morning we left Tumkur.

What, recount all my experiences from scratch? Well, I would need at least a thousand nights for that. All right, now let's go to sleep. For God's sake move a little. Good night!

This story was first published as "Pishach" in the anthology *Visappu* (1954).

Tiger

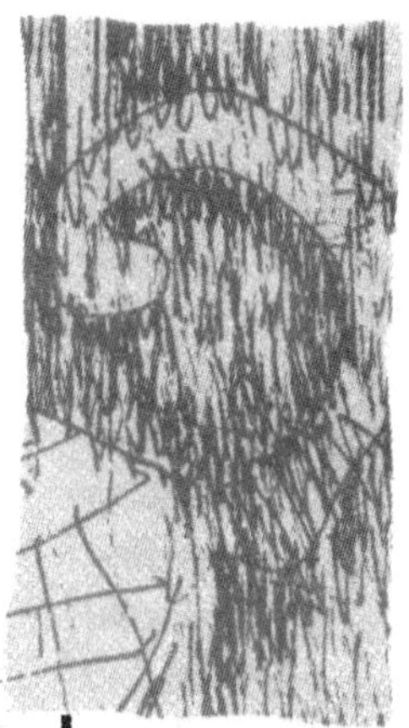

Tiger was untouched by the famine that had reduced most people in the country to mere skin and bones. Lucky dog!

In repose, one could mistake him for a bulging bundle wrapped in a blanket. He was a mongrel pup, littered in a city gutter. He knew nothing about his antecedents. Ever since he could remember, the police station and its precincts had been his home. Since his childhood, he had romped around in its courtyard, with its square patch of sky above.

Clever enough to distinguish between the policemen and the inmates of the lockup, Tiger knew each inhabitant of the police station. He displayed a certain partiality for the Inspector. The prisoners too did not fail to comment on the similarity between the Inspector's harsh eyes and the expression in Tiger's reddish brown eyes. In fact, they believed that expression to be characteristic of policemen in general.

Tiger categorized all the inmates of the lockup generically as "prisoners," without making any distinction between the murderer, the petty thief and the political détenu. As far as he was concerned, mankind consisted of only two kinds of people – policemen and convicts.

There were forty-five inmates in each of the different lockups. It was immaterial to Tiger that the four special inmates of a particular lockup were political activists. What he saw was that they all lived in the same foul-smelling infernos that admitted neither light nor fresh air.

translated by
Vanajam Ravindran

These pale-faced creatures, unshaven, bitten by bugs, clad in foul rags, existed in abject misery. They had become insensitive to both light and darkness. The offensive smell rising from the lockups was strong enough to corrode their human hearts. But strangely, the prisoners were unaffected by the stench. Their one thought, day in and day out, was food. An insatiable hunger gnawed at their bellies at all times. They would go to sleep so that they could receive their share of rice gruel in the morning, and having eaten it, they would wait for the midday meal, and then the food served at sundown.

All the inmates of the lockup also eagerly waited to be sentenced and sent to jail. They certainly did not have any hopes of acquittal and of being found innocent of the charges framed against them. The jail is the prisoners' heaven, the lockup his hell.

Tiger, who freely sauntered around the lockup or sometimes lounged at the door, was the object of seething resentment and rage. Each prisoner's heart conveyed its emotion through his eyes. All this did not bother Tiger.

During the Inspector's lunch, Tiger would keep guard at the door. After a heavy meal and a belch of contentment, the Inspector would pick up the folded banana leaf and leave it in front of Tiger. Enough to feed a man, the sight of the leftovers made the inmates salivate. Tiger would promptly gobble it all up.

After a nap in the cool arbour of the station yard, Tiger would present himself before the lockup door, the expression in his eyes suggestive of a smile – as if to say that he knew all their secrets. But most of the charges against the prisoners were false, fabricated by the Inspector and the policemen after receiving bribes.

A person once found guilty of theft is held responsible for just about any theft for the rest of his life. Under pressure, he even confesses to crimes not committed by him. He testifies before the Magistrate too, because of the unnerving presence of the police in the court.

As for the policeman's plight, his monthly salary is less than one-thirtieth the amount fixed for the daily ration of one prisoner. How then does a policeman feed his family on the meagre salary without supplementing it with other sources of income?

Through the iron bars, the indignant prisoners would put out their hands and poke the well-fed Tiger, saying, "You have fattened on our food."

In reply, the dog would wag his tail and look at them, as if to say, "Yes, these are the ironies of life. And they are irrevocable."

Initially, some inmates complained that the food they got was less than what the government had stipulated for them. They demanded their rightful share. What they got was a shower of blows from the constables and kicks from the booted Inspector, who muttered under his breath, "What the government had stipulated! As if the government is your bloody father."

The prisoners retorted, "As if the government is anybody's bloody father. The government is Tiger." Was that an apt parallel though?

A potbellied hotel proprietor with a handlebar moustache supplied food to the prisoners. This man had started in a small way, but had prospered because of them. The Inspector and the Station Writer not only had coffee and regular meals at his hotel for free, but were also given a fixed sum of money by the proprietor. Any loss he incurred on this score was made good by cutting down on the prisoners' daily rations. Even if they were starved, who was to question him?

Anyone inclined to complain to the Magistrate would remember the Inspector's ruthless flogging and think the better of it. In the course of time, they stopped voicing their complaints altogether. But they avenged themselves on Tiger.

The Inspector wondered why the prisoners disliked the poor creature. At every available opportunity they tried to hurt him. And the dog would start whining the moment he sensed their intent. The

Inspector would promptly come out of his room, brandishing his cane and ask, "Which rascal is hurting Tiger? You curs, haven't I told you not to tease him? Now, whoever did it, stretch out your hand."

A hand would then appear through the iron bars. Gripping the fingers tight, the Inspector would strike on the forearm and the surroundings would ring with loud cries as blood streamed from the raw wounds.

Tiger would come and lick the floor clean of the splattered drops of blood with his tongue. This punishment made the prisoners only more determined to hurt Tiger. And they repeated their folly, in spite of the fact that most of them had, some time or the other, been punished for hurting Tiger. The dog had a tendency to provoke such ire.

Tiger was a coward! He seldom left the precincts of the police station. If any stray dog entered the station yard, he would bark fiercely. At such times, his ferocity compared with that of a tiger. But on the rare occasions he came upon some miserable pye-dog outside his domain, he would beat a hasty retreat with his tail between the hind legs!

Witnessing one such scene, a political prisoner remarked, "Here comes our Inspector!" His companion philosophically commented that inside the heart of every one of them lurked an Inspector. This remark now triggered off a heated argument between him and three others.

As the debate reached its climax, the Inspector turned up unexpectedly and inquired what the commotion was all about. They said nothing. The Inspector got the sentry to open the door and announced the welcome news that they had visitors. The philosopher's companions had come with lots of oranges and other eatables. Two of the oranges were promptly sampled by the Inspector. The rest of the food was consumed by the inmates as they chatted.

The visitors had no fresh news to give them. The news they brought was all too familiar – about the war, rising prices and the famine. The prisoner who had started the argument said that the famine had affected them too. The surprised visitors remarked, "You? Aren't you the fortunate ones – well-fed, untouched by the problems of the world outside?"

Pointing to Tiger who was at the door, the philosopher said, "If only we were as fortunate as that dog!" Everyone, including the Inspector, laughed.

That evening, these prisoners could not do justice to the food served to them as their stomachs were full. They collected the leftovers and placed it in front of the lockup for those who had already been shut in.

From behind the bars, twenty-two inmates stared greedily at the spread before them. As one of them gingerly pulled at the banana leaf through the bars, a few morsels fell on the floor. In an instant, Tiger was there to lick up the morsels.

While one of them served, the others remained seated. There wasn't even a scoopful for everyone. Five people were served in this manner.

Meanwhile, Tiger had started licking up whatever curry had fallen on the floor and the bars of the lockup door. An inmate kicked him on his face and he yelped as if his life was in danger. The sentry came running, followed by a few policemen and the Inspector.

The Inspector forced the prisoners to put back the measly quantity of rice from the scoop of their palms on to the banana leaf. It was like plucking out their hearts. That done, the leaf was placed before Tiger.

Not satisfied with having snatched the morsels almost from their mouths, the Inspector got the sentry to unlock the door, went in and showered blows and kicks on all the twenty-two prisoners in the lockup.

Around ten at night, the police station echoed with ear-splitting yelps. Tiger was screaming without respite. Everyone awoke to his agonized cries. A sentry came running to the spot. He saw two inmates forcing Tiger's head through the bars into the lockup. He was able to identify one of the two as an accused in a theft case.

The Inspector got this inmate out of the lockup and started raining violent blows, kicks and punches on him. Blood gushed out of the prisoner's mouth and formed a tiny red pool on the ground. A tooth too had fallen there. Tiger again came and licked the floor clean. The entire scene was witnessed by nine policemen and forty-five prisoners.

"Who was the other chap?" the Inspector asked the first culprit. But he would not reply. His legs were then pulled through the iron bars and tied together. The Inspector started lashing the soles with all his strength. As blood spurted from the gashes, Tiger licked the drops with his rough tongue.

The man lay still. Unconscious.

———————————

"Tiger" was first published in the anthology *Janmadinam* (1945).

Ettukali Mammoonhu

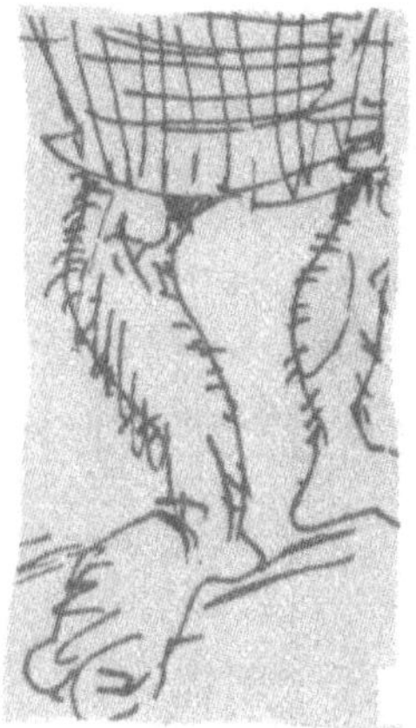

Somewhere, some woman conceives and I am held responsible!" exclaimed Ettukali Mammoonhu, pretending to be offended. He was actually trying hard to conceal his pride.

I must tell you that, till then, he had never had the confidence to boast like this.

Ettukali Mammoonhu was called so because he looked like a spider, an ettukali. Short-statured, with a small head, the one endowment he could boast of was his moustache. He let it hang a foot long on either side. There was a general complaint that he would let this appendage rub against the women he passed by. People said he was impotent, a secret that the women of the neighbourhood too knew. How they knew about this, nobody could tell.

"Coat Mammoonhu" was another of his names. This was because, while playing cards, Mammoonhu would invariably ask, "Do you have a coat?" If one wanted any service from him, he had to be respectfully addressed as "Coat Sahib." But in the prison records, he featured as "Ettukali Mammoonhu."

Mammoonhu wanted to participate in the adventures and experiences of the notorious rogues Anavari Raman Nair, Ponkurissu Thoma and others like them. But the poor fellow was not considered important enough to belong to that hierarchical order. Even the gambler Ottakkannan Pokker and the pickpocket Mandan Muthapa ignored him and treated him like a worm.

translated by
Vanajam Ravindran

PAUL KALLANODE

Judging by his looks, one may assume that, in the past, Ettukali Mammoonhu had been a comparatively better-looking spider. He was fond of everybody and ready to do anything for others – sweep and clean Muthapa's tea shop, also split firewood for him, polish the two constables's belts and the metal numbers on their topees till they glittered like gold. He even cleaned the lockup room of the police station. Yet nobody liked him. In a dismissive tone, they would say, "Hah, Mammoonhu!"

In this routine state of affairs, something eventful happened.

One day, Anavari Raman Nair was on his way to Muthapa's tea shop. Someone called out to him, "Hey, Anavari!"

This worthy turned back to respond. To his consternation, he saw that it was Mammoonhu. Needless to say, Anavari Raman Nair was furious. He did not tolerate such liberties even from distinguished people. Besides, in his own reckoning none of them was his equal. The few whose privilege it was to call him with such familiarity were Ponkurissu Thoma, Ottakkannan Pokker, Janab Mandan Muthapa, the two wily constables and the present narrator. And of course, some others who had all gone underground.

So infuriated was Anavari Raman Nair that he could have throttled Mammoonhu. But before anything as dire as that could happen, Ettukali Mammoonhu came close and said, "Do you know what has happened?"

He then whispered to him the amazing secret.

Stunned, Anavari asked, "Really?"

"Yes, it's true!" affirmed Mammoonhu, twirling the ends of his moustache.

The two walked towards Muthapa's tea shop. The moment he saw Thoma, Mammoonhu called out, "Hey, Ponkurissu, have you heard about this?"

Like Anavari Raman Nair, Ponkurissu Thoma felt an urge to thrash

Mammoonhu for his insolence. But before he could do so, Anavari whispered the secret to him and, with utter astonishment, Ponkurissu asked, "Ai, Ettukali, is this a fact?"

Twirling the ends of his moustache, Mammoonhu said, in a surprisingly controlled tone, "This bastard is capable of that and much more."

When they finally reached the tea shop, they saw that everyone who was anyone had congregated there – Ottakkannan Pokker, Mandan Muthapa and the two sly constables. Ettukali Mammoonhu revealed the precious secret to all of them. Taken aback, they too chorused, "Is this true, is this true?"

Mammoonhu said nothing. A smile played on his lips as he observed a meaningful silence. Muthapa then said, "Let me treat you to a cup of tea, Mammoonhu." Promptly came Pokker's offer to buy the hero two pieces of puttu. The curry to go with it was at Anavari's expense and Ponkurissu was to pay for the two bananas. The two constables contributed a vada and a sukhiyan.

Puffing on a beedi and enjoying the treat, Ettukali Mammoonhu straightaway became a member of their distinguished circle. In a moment, the news of his bravado spread all over the neighbourhood. He became famous as a real man. Wherever women gathered, they whispered about his daring act. "This Ettukali Mammoonhu is great!"

But what was this act of daring that everyone was talking about, the act that had won Ettukali Mammoonhu instantaneous fame? Let me slow down the pace of this narrative a little and take you back in time.

Two-and-a-half miles away from the spot, lived Undakkannan Andru, the greatest miser of the area. The path to his house was tortuous, the ground uneven and full of pits and hollows. Then you reached the slope of a hill where there was a small house with a thatched roof. This was Andru's house.

One of the most prosperous people around, Andru did not believe in charity. He neither gave loans nor lent money on interest. No one knew where all his money was hidden. Twice Anavari and Ponkurissu had attempted to burgle the house, but they could not find even one box. People in the locality firmly believed that it was buried in some secret place. But why should we talk about that and waste our time since it is not our problem at the moment.

After his mother died, Andru was in a fix. There was no one to do the household chores. To tide over the problem, he brought a young girl to work for him. Her name was Khadijumma. Her monthly salary was two annas, equivalent to our current twelve paise. Those were the days before the existence of workers' unions.

After a couple of months Andru started feeling distressed at the thought of having to part with so much money. This was how he calculated the salary he paid Khadijumma – one-and-a-half rupees per year, that would mean fifteen rupees in ten years and one hundred and fifty in ten decades. He shuddered at this appalling figure.

Promptly Andru summoned a musaliyar to perform his nikaah, and Khadijumma became his wedded wife.

Andru was relieved that he would not have to pay for her services any longer. As her husband, he was also free to beat her up any time he felt like it. And if anybody questioned him, he could always say, "Shut up you rascal! Don't I have the right to beat my own wife?"

But Andru's problems did not end there, alas!

Khadijumma started bearing children – three babies in three successive years. During the period of her confinement, she was in no condition to fetch and carry.

Andru soon found a way to surmount this problem as well. A relative of Khadijumma's, a nubile girl of nineteen – Thachi – was brought to work for them, on a monthly salary of one-and-a-half annas.

After two months, Thachi became pregnant. Nobody knew how.

It was around this time that Mammoonhu proudly said, "I am responsible for Thachi's condition!"

But though Mammoonhu went about flouting his active part in the great event, Thachi resolutely denied it, saying that no one was involved.

The worthies of this world have invented various ways to extract the truth from women in such situations. There is even a book on this subject, enumerating the methods.

In Andru's view, however, the three most effective ones were sprinkling pepper in the woman's eyes, bruising her all over the body and applying a paste of chilli and salt into the wounds and, lastly, scorching her palms with red hot embers.

Andru, miser that he was, found the last of these the most acceptable, for the simple reason that he did not have to part with pepper, salt or chillies. Andru himself administered the punishment.

As the hot embers burned her palm, Thachi cried out with pain, but nevertheless swore by everything sacred to her, "Aah! Nobody."

Andru was at his wits' end. He did not know what step to take next.

"Perhaps it is some illness," suggested his wife.

For several days, Andru's mind revolved round Thachi's pregnancy and illness. But as the days went by, he forgot all about the problem and became engrossed in his profitable jaggery business.

Let me give you a tip in case you have intentions of emulating Andru and getting rich through the jaggery trade. All you need to do is buy substandard jaggery at a phenomenally low price. Then mix it well with bran and oil cakes and make a thick syrup. When it acquires a thick consistency, pour the mixture into tiny coconut shells. Later, you can remove the hardened cakes from the shells and display them for sale as "little jaggery cakes."

But the matter at hand now is Thachi's pregnancy. Eleven months passed and yet the baby was not born! One day Andru called in a vaidya who owed him nearly eleven-and-a-half annas and, cursing him, got him to examine Thachi. The vaidya gave her some medicines, and declared she was not pregnant.

At this point, we must go back to Ettukali Mammoonhu, who will have to chronicle for us what happened subsequently.

One day, as Anavari was on his way to Muthapa's tea shop, Mammoonhu called out to him in a plaintive tone and said, "Hey Anavari, you know what has happened? They have killed my baby."

Anavari was stunned. Meeting Ponkurissu Thoma on their way, Mammoonhu broke the sad news to him as well, "They've killed my darling son."

In silence, the three walked up to Muthapa's shop. With his voice trembling and tears streaming down his cheek, Mammoonhu said, "Ai Muthapa, do you know something? They have killed my precious, darling son."

The terrible news reduced Muthapa to silence too. Soon one-eyed Pokker and the two constables heard about this high-handed act as well. They discussed every aspect of the issue, but could find no solution.

Ettukali Mammoonhu could control himself no longer. Fired by an uncontrollable rage, he announced, "I'll burn the entrails of the bastard who killed my son."

. Pacifying the Spider, one of the constables advised, "Be patient." The eldest son of Andru's father's second wife's sister's brother-in-law was a head constable. Naturally the two constables wouldn't go along with Mammoonhu's resolve to burn Andru's entrails – a justifiable one though. Here we have a glaring example of the abuse of official authority, the unity of officialdom.

But then what should Mammoonhu and his companions do about Andru?

As the days passed in gloom and uncertainty, Mammoonhu suddenly turned up at Muthapa's tea shop one day with some more shocking news. All of us were there when Mammoonhu asked us, "Have you heard the latest?"

A long pause followed the query.

Some great emotion held Ettukali Mammoonhu speechless. He looked the very image of the gods of Sorrow, Wrath and Pain all rolled into one.

At last, he burst into tears and, said in a quivering voice, "That round-eyed bastard destroyed my son first. Now he has married my wedded wife Thachi."

Students of history, here is a problem for you to mull over.

"Ettukali Mammoonhu" was first published in the anthology *Oru Bhagavad Gitayum Kure Mulakalum* (1967).

The invaluable moment

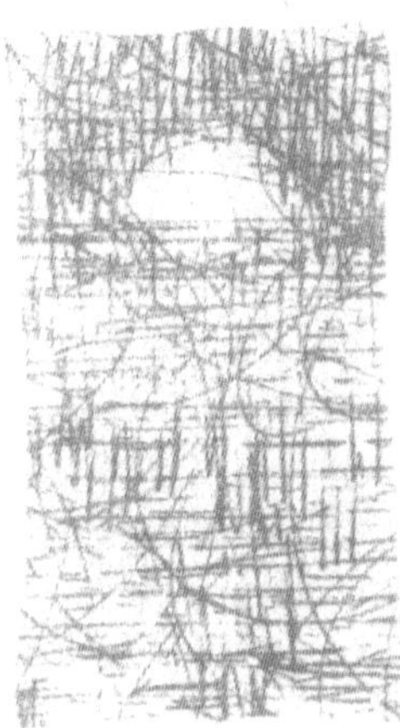

You and I - this reality is going to end any moment now. And then, you alone will remain.

You, alone.

The time for my final journey is fast approaching. The anguish welling up in my heart will burst forth like a rain-cloud and shatter my very being.

My friends are unaware of this sad fact. When they visit me, I crack jokes as usual and they cannot contain their laughter. To entertain them, I narrate humorous anecdotes. Laugh with them. They do not hear the rumbling notes of sadness behind my laughter.

Here I am. About to merge with nothingness.

Nothingness.

An inconsequential event - or is it a very important one? Something did happen. Is that what is important?

Anyway, I am that invaluable moment caught between two planes of existence - the past standing on the threshold of the present, and today which is going to merge completely into yesterday ... with the countless yugas ... the chaturyugas ... the eternal, the infinite ... the never-ending yesterday.

I bid farewell. It is all over.

No, it is going to be over.

From the next moment onwards I will be a part of all those countless yesterdays cast into oblivion.

Many of my friends have gone already. Where are they,

translated by
Vanajam Ravindran

I wonder, the multitudes who left before me? Memory constantly returns to the beginning.

The beginning ...

I feel as if I have finally reached the unknown boundary of eternity's mystery. Here it is! A resonant echo of Pranava's eternal jubilation.

Are you listening?

All this time, you loved me with boundless compassion. You suffered me. And you knew me. For you, I am an open book you can read and sense leisurely at your own convenience.

But you are still a great enigma for me. In all these years it has not been possible for me to know anything about you. Unawares, I loved you. Unawares, I hated you. Have I wantonly ever caused you pain? Even if I had, you loved me. Suffered me.

I have divulged many of my secrets to you. You have witnessed all my actions. Will you now make me a laughing stock?

Here, I leave now. Even as I go I continue to love you. When was it that you and I got to know each other? Or, did we ever know each other? I tried, though. Eventually, I learned only to love you. No, I never could comprehend anything clearly. Essentially, I knew nothing.

Alone I came into the world. Alone I go. The time for that journey is drawing near.

And you alone will now remain of the reality, *You and I*.

You, alone.

This story was first published as "Anarghanimisham" in 1946 in the anthology of the same name.

Basheer's
KERALA
KARNATAKA
TAMIL NADU
CANNANORE
TELLICHERRY
MAHE
KOZHIKODE (CALICUT)
BEYPORE

MUNNAR
COCHIN
VAIKOM
AALAPPUZHA (ALLEPPEY)
LAKSHADWEEP SEA
QUILON
THIRUVANANTHAPURAM (TRIVANDRUM)

VAIKOM MUHAMMAD BASHEER

1908   Basheer is born, probably on January 20, in the village of Thalayolaparambu in Vaikom (Travancore district), to Kunhachumma and Kayi Abdu Rahiman. Abdul Khader, Muhammad Hanifa, Abubacker, Fathima and Anumma are his siblings.
He attends the Malayalam school in Thalayolaparambu and later the Vaikom English School.

1924   Basheer "touches" Mahatma Gandhi when the latter visits Vaikom. Subsequently, Basheer runs away from home and comes in contact with Congress workers in Calicut.

1930   Basheer participates in the salt satyagraha at Calicut in April. Arrested and then tortured in various lockups, he is imprisoned in the Calicut and Cannanore jails.

1931-41   He is released from jail following the Gandhi-Irwin Pact which grants freedom to all political prisoners. He joins *Ujjevanam*, a paper which promotes terrorism. When the police siezes his anti-British writings, he leaves Kerala.
For seven years he wanders all over India and finally reaches the shores of Arabia. Basheer's first story, "Ente Thankam," is published in *Jayakesari*, a weekly.

1942   Basheer returns home, where an arrest warrant has been issued against him for a seditious article published in the *Rajyabhimani*. He is arrested by the Government of Travancore and sentenced to two-and-a-half years of rigorous imprisonment.

1943-45   He is released before the completion of his full term in jail. He works for some time for the magazine *Mangalodayam* in Trichur.

1944   He earns fame as a writer with the publication of his novella, *Balyakalasakhi*.

1947-48	Basheer works for *Jayakeralam* in Madras. His journalistic career prior to this includes stints on the editorial boards of *Sarasan, Pauranadam*, and *Bharatachandrika*. He returns from Madras and starts a book stall, the Circle Book House, in Ernakulam. Its name is later changed to Basheer's Book Stall.
1953-58	After a psychological setback, Basheer undergoes treatment at Ayurveda Mental Clinic in Trichur.
1958	He marries Fatima Bi on December 18. They have two children, Shahina and Anees.
1962	The Basheer family moves to a house on a two-acre plot of land in Beypore.
1970	The Kerala Sahitya Akademi confers a fellowship on him.
1972	Basheer receives a tamrapatra from the Government of India for his involvement in the freedom struggle.
1981	He receives the Kerala Sahitya Akademi Fellowship again.
1982	Basheer is honoured with the Padma Shri.
1983	The Abu Dhabi Malayalee Samaj Award is presented to Basheer.
1987	He receives the Samskara Deepam Award, and Calicut University honours him with a DLitt.
1992	He is presented the Lalithambika Antharjanam and the Prem Nazir awards.
1993	Vallathol Puraskaram and the Muttathu Varki Award are conferred on him.
1994	Basheer receives the Jeddah Arangu Award.
1994	July 5: Basheer passes away.

$\mathcal{B}$IBLIOGRAPHY

The Works of Vaikom Muhammad Basheer

In Malayalam

1.	*Premalekhanam*	(Love Letter)	1943
2.	*Balyakalasakhi*	(Childhood Friend)	1944
3.	*Kathabeejam*	(The Germ of a Story)	1945
4.	*Janmadinam*	(Birthday)	1945
5.	*Ormakurippu*	(Memoirs)	1946
6.	*Anarghanimisham*	(The Invaluable Moment)	1946
7.	*Sabdangal*	(Voices)	1947
8.	*Viddikalute Swargam*	(The Fools' Paradise)	1948
9.	*N'te Uppooppakkoru Anadarnu*	(My Grandfather had an Elephant)	1951
10.	*Maranathinte Nizhalil*	(In the Shadow of Death)	1951
11.	*Mucheettukalikkarante Makal*	(The Card-sharper's Daughter)	1951
12.	*Pavapettavarute Vesya*	(The Prostitute for the Poor)	1952
13.	*Sthalathe Pradhana Divyan*	(The Superman of the Place)	1953
14.	*Anavariyum Ponkurissum*	(Anavari and Ponkurissu)	1953
15.	*Jeevita Nizhalpadukal*	(The Shadow Marks of Life)	1954
16.	*Viswavikhyatamaya Mookku*	(The World-renowned Nose)	1954

<table>
<tr><td>17.</td><td>*Visappu*</td><td>(Hunger)</td><td>1954</td></tr>
<tr><td>18.</td><td>*Pathummayute Adu*</td><td>(Pathumma's Goat)</td><td>1959</td></tr>
<tr><td>19.</td><td>*Mathilukal*</td><td>(Walls)</td><td>1965</td></tr>
<tr><td>20.</td><td>*Oru Bhagavad Gitayum Kure Mulakalum*</td><td>(One Bhagavad Gita and Many Breasts)</td><td>1967</td></tr>
<tr><td>21.</td><td>*Taraspeshyals*</td><td>(Tara Specials)</td><td>1968</td></tr>
<tr><td>22.</td><td>*Manthrika Poocha*</td><td>(The Magic Cat)</td><td>1968</td></tr>
<tr><td>23.</td><td>*Nerum Nunayum*</td><td>(The True and the False)</td><td>1969</td></tr>
<tr><td>24.</td><td>*Ormayute Arakal*</td><td>(Chambers of Memory)</td><td>1973</td></tr>
<tr><td>25.</td><td>*Anappoota*</td><td>(The Elephant's Hair)</td><td>1975</td></tr>
<tr><td>26.</td><td>*Chirikkunna Marappava*</td><td>(The Smiling Wooden Doll)</td><td>1975</td></tr>
<tr><td>27.</td><td>*Bhoomiyute Avakasikal*</td><td>(The Rightful Inheritors of the Earth)</td><td>1977</td></tr>
<tr><td>28.</td><td>*Anuragathinte Dinangal*</td><td>(The Days of Love)</td><td>1983</td></tr>
<tr><td>29.</td><td>*Bhargavinilayam*</td><td>(Bhargavi's House)</td><td>1985</td></tr>
<tr><td>30.</td><td>*M P Paul*</td><td>(M P Paul)</td><td>1991</td></tr>
<tr><td>31.</td><td>*Singiti Mungan*</td><td>(Singiti Mungan)</td><td>1991</td></tr>
<tr><td>32.</td><td>*Cheviyorkuka, Antima Kahalam*</td><td>(Listen, The Final Call)</td><td>1992</td></tr>
<tr><td>33.</td><td>*Basheer: Sampoorna Krithikal*</td><td>(Basheer: The Complete Works, two volumes)</td><td>1992</td></tr>
</table>

In English Translation

1. *Voices/The Walls*, trans V Abdulla, Sangam Books, Madras, 1976.

2. *The Magic Cat*, trans N Kunju, Kerala Sahitya Akademi, 1978.

3.   *"Me Grandad 'ad an Elephant!": Three Stories of Muslim Life in South India*, trans R E Asher et al, University of Edinburgh Press, 1980, and Penguin India, 1992.

4.   *The Love Letter and Other Stories*, trans V Abdulla, Sangam Books, Madras, 1983.

5.   *Poovan Banana and Other Stories*, trans V Abdulla, Orient Longman, Madras, 1994.

Some Important Works on Basheer

1.   *Cherukatha Innale Innu* (The Short Story: Yesterday and Today), M Achutan, NBS, Kottayam, 1973.

2.   *Novelukalilude* (Through the Novels), K P Sharatchandran, NBS, Kottayam, 1973.

3.   *Vaikom Muhammad Basheerinte Novelukal* (The Novels of Vaikom Muhammad Basheer), M N Karasseri – a collection of articles published as a series under the title *Nanmayute Velicham* (The Light of Goodness) in the weekly *Chandrika*, Kozhikode, September 1975 to July 1976.

4.   *Basheerinte Katha Sahityam* (Basheer's Fictional Works), Vijayalayam Jayakumar, NBS, Kottayam, 1978.

5.   *Basheerinte Lokam* (The World of Basheer), ed M M Basheer, D C Books, Kottayam, 1985.

6.   *Sultan Paranha Kathakal* (The Tales the Sultan Told), Hyderali Tatapuram, Siyad Books, Cochin, 1986.

7.   *Malayalathinte Basheer* (Malayalam's Basheer), Paul Manalil, Current Books, Kottayam, 1988.

8.   *Anughraheetanaya Basheer* (Basheer, the Blessed), K M Tharakan, Janata Services, Cochin, 1989.

9.   *Uppuppante Kuyyanakal* (Grandpa's Ant Lions), Raghunathan Nair, NBS, Kottayam, 1989.

10. *Basheerinte Airavathangal* (Basheer's White Elephants), E M Ashraf, Current Books, Kottayam, 1990.

11. *Basheerinte Jeevitavum Krithikalum* (Basheer's Life and Works, PhD thesis) Jamaluddin Kunhu, Department of Malayalam, Calicut University, Kozhikode, 1991.

12. *Marubhoomikal Pookkumbol* (When Deserts Bloom), M N Vijayan, Kalakshetram: The Publishing People, Kasarkode, 1993.

13. *Basheer Varthamanathinte Bhavi* (Basheer: The Future of the Present), ed M K Sanu, Asayam Books, Kozhikode, 1994.

14. *Vaikom Muhammad Basheer*, E M Ashraf, D C Books, Kottayam, 1994.

15. *Balyakalasakhi Suvarna Jubilee Pathippu* (Golden Jubilee Issue of *Balyakalsakhi*), ed M M Basheer, D C Books, Kottayam, 1994.

16. *Iruttil Urangathirikkunna Oral* (The Man Who Kept Awake in the Dark), Vijayakrishnan, Current Books, Kottayam, 1995.

17. *Mumbe Natanna Basheer* (Basheer, the Pioneer) ed Paul Manalil, Current Books, Kottayam, 1995.

18. *Atum Manvshyarum* (Goats and Humans), ed M A Rahman, Current Books, Kottayam, 1995.

19. *Balyakalasakhi: Kannunir Pottichiriyakkunna Kala* (*Balyakalasakhi*: The Art of Transforming Tears into Laughter), ed Paul Manalil, In Print.

THE CONTRIBUTORS

Geeta Dharmarajan is a writer for children and adults. Editor of *Katha Prize Stories*, an annual anthology of the best of Indian regional fiction in translation, Geeta also writes for and edits *Tamasha!*, a fun and development magazine for first-generation schoolgoers. She started Katha in 1988 and is its Executive Director.

Vanajam Ravindran retired as Reader from the Faculty of English of Lady Shri Ram College for Women, University of Delhi. An occasional writer of articles and reviews, she has contributed to journals like *In-between* and the *Indian Review of Books*. Her translations from Malayalam have been published in *Indian Literature, Katha Prize Stories 5* and *The Wordsmiths*. For the last book, she has also interviewed M T Vasudevan Nair. Dr Ravindran won the Katha Award for Translation in 1995. She lives in Kozhikode.

M N Vijayan is a reputed critic and writer in Malayalam. He is the author of *Marubhoomikal Pookkumbol,* the first comprehensive study of Basheer's writings. A teacher of Malayalam, Prof Vijayan retired from Government Brennen College, Tellicherry in 1985. *A Critical Study of Kesari's Works* and *Kesari's Worlds* are some of his works in Malayalam. *Collected Speeches*, a collection of his speeches on Literature and allied subjects, is characterized by strong convictions that lend force to his writings. He is currently the president of the Purogamana Kala Sahitya Sangham, Kerala.

K M Sherrif has an MA in English from the University of Calicut and teaches English at the Narmada College of Science and Commerce, Zadeshwar, Gujarat. His areas of interest are translation and cultural studies, with special emphasis on popular culture. His translations in Malayalam, Gujarati and English have been published in reputed journals and magazines and he received the Katha Award for Translation in 1993. He introduced Gujarati Dalit literature into English for the first time in a special edition of *Indian Literature*

(January-February 1994) and his forthcoming publications are "Ekalavyas with Thumbs: Selections from Gujarati Dalit Literature" and "Games Gods Play," a translation of M Mukundan's award winning Malayalam novel, *Daivathinte Vikrithikal.*

Nivedita Menon, the winner of Katha's A K Ramanujan Award for Translation in 1994, is a lecturer in Political Science at Lady Shri Ram College for Women, Delhi University. She has completed her doctoral dissertation on the interaction between feminist and legal discourse in India and has several published articles in the field to her credit. She is currently Visiting Fellow at the Centre for the Study of Developing Societies, Delhi.

V C Harris has a PhD in English and teaches at the School of Letters, Mahatma Gandhi University, Kottayam. A translator and critic, he has several publications to his credit, both in English and Malayalam. He is the co-translator of *The Sandal Trees and Other Stories* by Kamala Das (Disha Books, 1995). He has also written and directed a television documentary, *Basheer: Images of Light,* which was telecast by Doordarshan and also selected for screening at important festivals such as the Bombay International Film Festival in 1996 and the International Video Film Festival held at Thiruvananthapuram in 1995.

Paul Kallanode is a poet, painter, sculptor and cartoonist. A member of the Kerala Sahitya Akademi and the Kerala Lalit Kala Akademi, he has participated in many national and state artist camps and exhibitions. His poems and cartoons appear frequently in the leading journals of Kerala. For his poetry, he was honoured with the Mahakavi Idassery Award in 1990 and the Kanakashree Award in 1995 of the Kerala Sahitya Akademi. He has also received the Indian Junior Chambers State Outstanding Young Person Award in 1991 and the Khozhikode IMA Award in 1996. He lives in Kozhikode where he teaches in St Joseph's Boys' High School.

Punalur Rajan is a professional photographer. He has been associated with Basheer ever since the writer settled in Beypore. Basheer was a sort of godfather to him. The young photographer has captured the writer in many moods and frames. He speaks of Basheer as a humanitarian and a very humane person, full of idiosyncracies and a special warmth. Punalur Rajan lives and works in Kozhikọde.

Taposhi Ghoshal has graduated from the Delhi College of Art. A well-known freelance designer and illustrator based in Delhi, her work has been featured in a number of art exhibitions in the city.

ABOUT KATHA

Katha, a registered nonprofit organization set up in September 1989, works in the areas of education, publishing and community development and endeavours to spread the joy of reading, knowing and living amongst adults and children. Our main objective is **to enhance the pleasures of reading for children and adults,** for experienced readers as well as for those who are just beginning to read. Our attempt is also to stimulate an interest in lifelong learning that will help the child grow into a confident, self-reliant, responsible and responsive adult, as also to help break down gender, cultural and social stereotypes, encourage and foster excellence, applaud quality literature and translations in and between the various Indian languages and work towards community revitalization and economic resurgence. The two wings of Katha are **Katha Vilasam** and **Kalpavriksham**

KATHA VILASAM, the Story Research and Resource Centre, was set up to foster and applaud quality Indian literature and take these to a wider audience through quality translations and related activities like **Katha Books, Academic Publishing,** the **Katha Awards** for fiction, translation and editing, **Kathakaar** – the Centre for Children's Literature, **Katha Barani** – the Translation Resource Centre, the **Katha Translation Exchange Programme, Translation Contests. Kanchi –** the Katha National Institute of Translation promotes translation through **Katha Academic Centres** in various Indian universities, **Faculty Enhancement Programmes** through Workshops, seminars and discussions, **Sishya** – Katha Clubs in colleges, **Storytellers Unlimited** – the art and craft of storytelling and **KathaRasa** – performances, art fusion and other events at the Katha Centre.

KALPAVRIKSHAM, the Centre for Sustainable Learning, was set up to foster quality education that is relevant and fun for children from nonliterate families, and to promote community revitalization and economic resurgence work. These goals crystallized in the development of the following areas of activities. **Katha Khazana** which includes **Katha Student Support Centre, Katha Public School, Katha School of Entrepreneurship, KITES** – the Katha Information Technology and eCommerce School, **Iccha Ghar – The Intel Computer Clubhouse @ Katha, Hamara Gaon** and **The Mandals** – Maa, Bapu, Balika, Balak and Danadini, **Shakti Khazana** was set up for skills upgradation and income generation activities comprising the Khazana Coop. **Kalpana Vilasam** is the cell for regular research and development of teaching/learning materials, curricula, syllabi, content comprising **Teacher Training, TaQeEd — The Teachers Alliance for Quality eEducation. Tamasha's World!** comprises **Tamasha! the Children's magazine,** *Dhammakdhum! www.tamasha.org* and ANU – Animals, Nature and YOU!

BE A FRIEND OF KATHA!

If you feel strongly about Indian literature, you belong with us! KathaNet, an invaluable network of our friends, is the mainstay of all our translation-related activities. We are happy to invite you to join this ever-widening circle of translation activists. Katha, with limited financial resources, is propped up by the unqualified enthusiasm and the indispensable support of nearly 5000 dedicated women and men.

We are constantly on the lookout for people who can spare the time to find stories for us, and to translate them. Katha has been able to access mainly the literature of the major Indian languages. Our efforts to locate resource people who could make the lesser-known literatures available to us have not yielded satisfactory results. We are specially eager to find Friends who could introduce us to Bhojpuri, Dogri, Kashmiri, Maithili, Manipuri, Nepali, Rajasthani and Sindhi fiction.

Do write to us with details about yourself, your language skills, the ways in which you can help us, and any material that you already have and feel might be publishable under a Katha programme. All this would be a labour of love, of course! But we do offer a discount of 20% on all our publications to Friends of Katha.

Write to us at –
Katha
A-3 Sarvodaya Enclave
Sri Aurobindo Marg   Call us at: 652 4350, 652 4511
New Delhi 110 017   or E-mail us at: info@katha.org